LOVE AT THE
LIGHTHOUSE

KAY CORRELL

ROSE QUARTZ PRESS

Published by Rose Quartz Press

061917

This book is dedicated to my father, a man lost and locked in the frightening world of Alzheimer's. If I could make a wish on Lighthouse Point, my fervent wish would be that they find the cure for this horrible disease.

Find more information on all my books at
kaycorrell.com

COMFORT CROSSING ~ THE SERIES
The Shop on Main - Book One
The Memory Box - Book Two
The Christmas Cottage - A Holiday Novella
(Book 2.5)
The Letter - Book Three
The Christmas Scarf - A Holiday Novella
(Book 3.5)
The Magnolia Cafe - Book Four
The Unexpected Wedding - Book Five

The Wedding in the Grove - (a crossover short story

between series - with Josephine and Paul from The Letter.)

LIGHTHOUSE POINT ~ THE SERIES
Wish Upon a Shell - Book One
Wedding on the Beach - Book Two
Love at the Lighthouse - Book Three
Cottage near the Point - Book Four
Return to the Island - Book Five

INDIGO BAY ~ A multi-author sweet romance series
Sweet Sunrise - Book Three
Sweet Holiday Memories - A short holiday story
Sweet Starlight - Book Nine

Sign up for my newsletter at my website *kaycorrell.com* to make sure you don't miss any new releases or sales.

CHAPTER 1

S usan Hall sat at the desk in the office of Belle Island Inn. She stared at the screen, wanting to swat the computer monitor, as if that would help anything. Why did this software program insist on always having to prove its superiority over her?

She rolled her shoulders forwards and back, trying to release the tension. It's not like she was going to be able to make the program say they had more money than they really did. The negative number blinked wickedly at her from the screen, then as if to mock her, the computer shut down without so much as a goodbye.

"Seriously?" Susan smacked her hands on the desk in exasperation, jumped up from the desk, and stalked over to the window. She tugged the window open and let a fresh ocean breeze cool the room and toss her short curls around her face, which just reminded her she needed to get a haircut soon. Great, she'd put it on the ever-growing to-do list.

She was not going to bother her son, Jamie. He and Cindy had just gotten back from their honeymoon, and he didn't need any extra responsibility right now. He should be basking in his newly-wedded bliss.

She sighed a long whoosh of breath that carried her frustration and defeat across the room. Maybe she'd go take a long beach walk and see if the computer would cooperate when she returned. Or maybe she'd just chuck the thing in the trash.

You know, if they could afford to throw the outdated machine away.

She spun around and strode out into the lobby. Dorothy looked up from where she was working the reception desk. "You okay?"

Susan grimaced. "Let's just say the computer won this round."

"Want me to see if I can find Jamie? He can charm any computer into submission."

"Find me for what?" Her son came walking into the lobby. His eyes sparkled with happiness. Susan loved to see him in such good spirits these days.

Cindy had been the best thing to happen to this family in a long time.

She wouldn't be the one to bring down his mood. "It's nothing."

"It's something, I can tell from looking at you."

"I don't want to bother you. Just computer problems. I'll work on it some more this afternoon."

"I'll take a look at it. That computer seems to shut down more than stay on. We really need to replace it."

"Put it on the list." Susan bit her lip, unwilling to go down the pity-party path again.

"I'll go coax it back to life." Jamie winked.

"Thanks, you do seem to have the special touch when it comes to that cranky machine." So much for a walk. She wasn't going to send him in there to fight the good fight while she strolled along the beach. Though even if he got it working again, she was pretty certain it wasn't going to give her the answer she wanted. The answer that said they had money in the bank and everything was going to be all right.

Adam Lyons sat at his modern, polished, mahogany desk in the high-rise office in downtown Atlanta.

He flipped open his laptop and quickly logged in. His laptop was the newest, top-of-the-line machine. His boss spared no expense with his company. Adam knew he'd been lucky to land this job.

Now he just needed to prove himself.

He wanted to review the files and all the information he had before he left on his business trip. He was determined to make this deal go through—a hefty bonus was riding on the outcome. Heck, maybe even his job was riding on it. He wasn't going to let his boss down. Or himself, or anyone. He was done with that. His boss was absolutely driven about acquiring this property, and Adam was just the man to close the deal.

He glanced at his watch, then back to the screen. He looked up the history of the property and owners. He poured over what public records he could find, then did a quick search on the internet.

From what he could tell, this should be a no-brainer deal. Get in, make an offer—as low as possible—and get out. Hopefully, it would all go just that quickly so he could get right back home. He didn't want to be away for long. He'd already seen what happened when he left for any length of time and it wasn't going to happen again.

Adam crossed the wooden floor of the lobby of Belle Island Inn. He could see signs of wear, both inside and out. But the place looked clean, and the parking lot was partially filled, even during this off-season. As he'd walked inside, he'd noted the front porch could use a fresh coat of paint, even if the windows were sparkly clean.

A young man looked up from the desk and smiled. "May I help you?"

"Yes, I'm checking in. Adam Lyons."

"Welcome, Mr. Lyons. Glad to have you."

The young man punched the keys on the keyboard. Adam noted it was an old, thicker monitor, and the man seemed to be clicking around a lot to get the computer to give him what he wanted.

"Ah, there you are. It doesn't say how long you're staying?"

"About three days if all goes well."

"Business or pleasure?"

"Ah, pleasure." Adam had a momentary twinge of remorse for the lie, but didn't want to tip anyone off about why he was here. He couldn't imagine a lot of people came to the island on business.

"Okay." The man punched in some more information, frowned, and clicked more keys. He looked up and smiled. "Having a bit of a problem with the computer today. No worries. I've got it now."

Adam took in the ancient printer sitting on a ledge behind the man. It looked like they weren't investing much in technology here.

"Okay, here's your key." The man handed him a regular key with a plastic diamond-shaped key fob. "I'm Jamie, by the way. Let me know if I can do anything for you. Oh, and sorry, but the elevator isn't working today. You'll need to take the stairs to the third floor. Or, if that's a problem I could move you to the first floor."

"No, the third floor is fine."

Adam took the key and turned from the desk. Jamie. That was one of the owners of the inn. Seemed pretty young to be running it. Maybe that was part of the reason the inn was failing, but that was fine as far as Adam was concerned. A young owner might be more willing to take the money offered and run with it.

Things were looking good so far.

Adam smiled as he climbed the three flights of stairs up to his room. He unlocked the door and pushed inside. He didn't know what he'd been expecting, but the room was large, meticulously appointed, clean, and comfortable looking. It was exactly the type of place he'd like to stay if he were actually vacationing. As if he ever vacationed. He couldn't imagine how he'd ever pull off one again. There were just too many responsibilities.

He crossed over and opened the French doors to the balcony. A wide expanse of white sand and turquoise water stretched before him. It was a fabulous view. No wonder his boss was so interested in the property. There were no luxury resorts on the island, and with this purchase and the other properties they'd already acquired next door and across the street, they'd have something that could really work.

He just needed to close the deal on purchasing the inn.

CHAPTER 2

The next morning Adam walked out the front door of the inn and headed in the direction the woman at the reception desk had pointed him. He wanted to see the town, and the friendly lady at the desk had suggested he try a place called The Sweet Shoppe for his breakfast.

The warm morning weather was a perfect companion for his mood, hopeful, determined, and pretty sure of himself, if he did say so himself.

He stopped at the end of the road and looked both ways, trying to remember which way he was supposed to go.

"Are you lost?" A woman with a quick smile and golden red curls walked up to him.

He smiled back at her. "I am. Just a bit. I'm trying to find The Sweet Shoppe."

"Well, you're in luck. I'm headed there now. Come on, I'll show you the way."

"That would be great, thanks." He fell into step with the woman.

"Julie, the owner of the shop, is the best baker on the island. She always has something scrumptious for breakfast. I'm hoping for peach muffins today. I highly recommend them."

"I'll remember that."

"She's a friend of mine. I'm meeting her and another friend for coffee."

"So you live here?"

"Moved here a few years back. I've visited for years though. My brother used to live here."

Before he had a chance to ask about her brother, the woman moved on to another question. "So are you vacationing here?"

Once again he felt a twinge for his white lie. Well, outright lie, but it's not like he could say he was here for business, because what if someone asked what business? "Ah, yes. A brief break for a bit." He changed the subject to avoid his guilty conscience. "It's a nice island. I didn't know the ocean was such a deep shade of turquoise here, different shades of it as the sun bounces across it."

The last time he'd been to the ocean—and it had been years ago—he'd gone to the Outer Banks. The waves had been wild, and the sea and sand a darker color than here.

"It is a pretty island. I admit, I love living here." Her eyes lit up when she said it.

It was obvious she meant every word. Her smile spread across her entire face and her sky-blue eyes charmed him. It had been a while since he'd really even noticed a woman. Maybe this island was his lucky charm. Maybe his life would turn around. If he got the bonus and could get things settled in Atlanta, maybe he'd even start dating when he returned to Georgia. Maybe.

"I can see why you like living here." He *could* see why someone would enjoy it. The town had a picturesque quality to it, one his boss surely would use to his advantage. He'd have to take some more photos of the town and the island to include with his report. It would be a good idea to get a head start on marketing ideas, too.

"Where are you from?" The woman interrupted his thoughts.

Good, he could answer that truthfully. "I'm from Atlanta."

"Ah, I lived there for a while. It's a nice city. Big, though. Do you like living there?"

"I guess so." He hadn't really thought about it. It was just where he had ended up. And now he stayed there because... well, because he had to. He held back a sigh and put all the complications of his life out of his mind. Or tried to.

"Here we are." The woman stopped at the door of the bakery.

He opened the door for her, and his senses were immediately assaulted with the delicious aroma of cinnamon and all sorts of delectable scents.

"Thanks for the guided tour." He smiled at her.

"You're more than welcome. Enjoy your stay."

She went over to join two women at a table by the window, and he took a table in the corner, pulling out a notebook and jotting down some quick thoughts while he waited for his peach muffin.

"So, who was that?" Tally asked as Susan slipped into the chair beside her.

"I don't know. A lost visitor looking for The Sweet Shoppe, so I walked with him here."

"He's good looking." Her friend Julie eyed the man.

"Aren't you engaged?" Susan poured herself a cup of coffee from the pot on the table.

"I am. But... I meant for you." Julie grinned.

"Not much reason to fall for someone here for a quick visit."

"You mean like I did for Reed?" Julie laughed. "And here he is staying on the island with me."

"That worked out well, now didn't?" Tally asked. "Did you set a wedding date yet?"

"No, not yet. But I'm about ready. I think."

"You're just letting that poor man sit and wait and wait." Tally shook her head. "You love him. He loves you. He's proven that by moving here instead of heading back to Seattle."

"I know... I just... I don't know *why* I haven't set a date." Julie shrugged.

"Look at Jamie and Cindy. They got engaged, planned a wedding, and were married within a month." Susan cocked an eyebrow.

"How are they doing?" Tally took a quick bite of the almond danish on her plate.

"They're doing great. I've never seen Jamie this happy. Cindy is all smiles these days, too. I do feel badly that we're all crowded into the cottage though. But we don't really have the funds now to get another place. Cindy and Jamie want to make it on their own without accepting any help from her father, so our income is just from the inn and Cindy's job." Susan sipped her coffee. "I offered to move into a room of the inn for a while—especially since it's off season—to give them some space, but they wouldn't hear of it. Maybe I should offer again. We do have that one room that we haven't renovated yet, so we rarely have anyone stay in it. I could move in there."

Just like that, her mind was made up. When she got back she was going to insist she move into the inn for a bit and let the newlyweds have some privacy. She could even paint the room while she was staying in it and refinish the floors. It was a plan. She enjoyed that kind of work and she'd have time while they were so slow.

"I can see by the set of your shoulders and the look in your eyes that you've decided." Tally tossed a small smile.

"I have. I'm going to move into that room this afternoon."

With that, Susan turned her attention to the plate of baked goods on the table. Time to make a decision on which delicious, calorie-laden, guilt-inducing goodie she'd have this morning. Afterwards she could pretend the walk back to the inn would burn off all the calories.

Susan pulled the door to her room at the inn closed and locked it. She refused to listen to Jamie and insisted on moving some of her things into the room in the inn. Jamie in turn had insisted she take the night off, and she'd decided he was right. She could use a break.

With a sudden swath of light, the door opened across from her room. The man from the walk to The Sweet Shoppe stood in the doorway.

He smiled at her. "So we meet again."

"It's you." Susan smiled at him.

"It *is* me." His friendly smile still lingered on his face. He paused for the slightest moment, she could see his hesitation, then he spoke again. "I was just going to eat dinner. Would you care to join me?"

Now she paused.

"I mean if you don't already have plans. I guess that was forward of me to ask." He backpedaled.

She made a spontaneous decision, which rarely —*okay never*—happened. "Yes, I'd like to go."

"Perfect."

"We can go to Magic Cafe if you'd like. One of my friends owns it."

"You have a lot of friends." He laughed.

"Well, two best ones, Julie and Tally."

"Off to Magic Cafe then." He held out an arm and motioned for her to show him the way.

She led the way out of the inn and onto the back deck. "Do you mind if we walk the beach way?"

"Fine by me." They both slipped off their shoes as they reached the sand and crossed to the water's edge.

They fell into step, the waves racing up the beach towards them, then rushing back into the ocean. She loved this time of day, this time of year. A warmth radiated through her when she thought of her good fortune these days. Jamie was happy, and though they didn't have extra in the bank, they somehow seemed to make ends meet. She took a quick look at the man walking beside her. And it was kind of nice to have a dinner companion for a change. Most of her meals involved just grabbing something at the inn and working right through mealtime.

She stopped and touched his arm, causing him to pause.

"You know, I don't even know your name." She looked up into his sea-blue eyes. What would Jamie say if he knew she was going to dinner with someone whose name she didn't even know? She was definitely rusty at this date thing. Was it a date if a stranger asked you to join him for dinner? She didn't know the answer to that.

He smiled and held out his hand. "Adam. Adam Lyons."

"Nice to meet you. I'm Susan. Susan Hall." She shook his strong, warm hand and a shiver ran up her spine.

He held her hand for just a moment longer than necessary and she swore she saw the faintest look of surprise cross his face. She finally took a breath when he released her.

CHAPTER 3

*S*usan Hall?

With that, his heart plummeted. That wasn't good. The first woman he'd taken the tiniest spark to in forever.

She was the other owner of the inn.

The one inn that he needed to buy and get the most rock-bottom price possible for his boss. The fates must be laughing at him.

He swallowed. "Susan. Okay, now we know each other's names." Only he knew who she was, what she did, and what the future held in store for her. Though, maybe she'd like to get rid of the inn? He held onto that hope and told himself not to get more involved with her, because he had to *not-exactly-cheat* her out of the inn. No, it wasn't that. It was just get the inn for the absolute best price possible.

But there was still the matter of dinner. He briefly considered saying he didn't feel well, but the other side of him decided he could have dinner and get her to talk about the inn. Maybe something in there would help him. Once again the pang of guilt stabbed at him. He didn't really like the person he was becoming regarding this sale, but he had no choice. He had to learn to get ruthless and had to make this deal happen.

"Well, Adam, let's go eat then." Susan turned and headed down the beach, and he walked silently beside her.

They crossed the sand and went onto the outside deck area of Magic Cafe. An older lady came over and gave Susan a big hug. "I didn't know you were coming tonight."

"Spur of the moment thing. Tally, this is Adam. Adam, Tally."

Adam held out his hand and felt the woman's firm handshake. "Nice to meet you."

"Just go on over to that open table." Tally pointed to the one table that was cleared on the edge of the deck. "I'll have your waitress bring over a menu."

Susan crossed over to the table and he held out

the chair for her to sit. She smiled at him in thanks. He took a seat across from her and browsed the menu the waitress brought him.

"You want to see the menu?" He held it out to Susan.

She laughed. "No, I have it memorized."

They placed their orders and an awkward silence hung between them, mostly filled with his guilt. He wasn't ready to confess he knew she was the inn's owner. That was a bit too stalker-ish.

Then his mind jumped. Why was she staying at the inn? Did she actually live there? Or maybe she was just coming out of the room after checking on something. His mind clicked into business mode and he made a mental note to see if the inn had any long-term residents that they'd need to deal with.

Susan broke the silence. "So, are you enjoying your stay at the inn?"

"I am, the place is great." He watched her face.

"Glad you like it. Actually, my son and I own it. I always like to hear that our guests are enjoying themselves."

"Do you like running it?" He squirmed self-consciously in his seat like a schoolboy caught cheating on an exam.

"I do. It's frustrating sometimes and things break and problems happen, but I do love the place.

Jamie is good at fixing things and we have started to get busier. We've even started having a bit of wedding business and that has really helped out."

"Really?" He let her continue.

"Honestly, it's been a bit of a struggle, but it's been great working with my son. He loves the place as much as I do." Susan's eyes lit up again in the way he'd already become used to when she talked about something she cared about. No denying that she was fond of the inn.

"We took it over after my brother died. He owned it before us and Jamie had worked at the inn during the summers when he was young, then came down here to help my brother when my brother got ill. I moved here to help Jamie after my brother passed away."

"I'm sorry to hear that. I mean, sorry about your brother."

"Thank you. He fought it hard, but it ended up that the cancer won." A hint of pain flashed across Susan's face. "Anyway, I came down here, and I've been here ever since. Slowly turning the business around. Love it here. Tally is a sharp businesswoman and has given me lots of advice. She's helped Julie with The Sweet Shoppe, too. It's all hard work, but I enjoy it." A hint of a smile spread across her face. "Most days."

The smile lingered. Her smile did something to him. Warmed him. Made him feel welcome. Made him feel guilty...

He held onto the fact that maybe if someone dropped an offer to buy the inn in her lap, she'd be pleased. But as he watched her face, he had a sinking feeling that she wasn't going to jump on just any offer. That maybe she wouldn't accept any offer at all. Maybe, just maybe, she loved the inn that much.

Which if that was true, he was in big, big trouble.

Tally took a break from the dinner rush and slipped into a seat at Susan and Adam's table. "Did you like your grouper?" She glanced at Adam's plate.

"I did. It was delicious."

Tally felt a smile spread across her face. She loved to hear that people enjoyed meals at her restaurant. "Glad you enjoyed it."

She turned to Susan. "So did you get moved into the inn?"

"I did. Jamie protested a bit, but helped me move some of my things." Susan turned to Adam. "My son just got married and he and I and his new wife were all living in the small cottage on the property. I decided that I'd move into the inn for a bit and give them some space. Besides, I'll do some updating to the room while I'm living there. It's one of the last rooms that needs new paint and the floors refinished."

Tally watched Adam as he listened to Susan. He listened almost a bit too intently, but maybe the man was just interested in Susan. And why not? Her friend was an interesting person.

She turned to look at Susan and stifled a grin. Ah, her friend had that look. Tally saw the sparks in Susan's eyes. Her friend was taken by this Adam fellow. Well, it would do Susan good to have a few dates and get a break from the grind of running the inn. Now that Jamie was back from his honeymoon, Susan should be able to sneak away for a few outings.

And what was it with her friends getting interested in guys who were just here temporarily?

"So, how long are you in town?" Tally asked Adam.

"I'm not sure. A few more days, I think."

Well, that wasn't really enough time for anything to develop, but at least it would give her friend a chance to go out.

"You should take Adam to see Lighthouse

Point." Might as well push that whole dating thing along.

Susan shot her a glance, then looked at Adam questioningly. "I could maybe find time tomorrow."

"I'd like that." Adam leaned forward. "I'd like that a lot."

"It's a date then." Tally sat back and grinned. Mission accomplished. Susan would take some time off and have some male companionship.

Susan cocked an eyebrow, obviously aware she'd been played, but she smiled.

Tally didn't figure that Susan minded her meddling in this case.

CHAPTER 4

The next morning Adam's cell rang while he was still at the need-coffee-to-wake-up stage. His boss.

He took a deep breath, "Good morning, sir."

"How are things there? Getting it all wrapped up? I have my lawyer ready to draw up the final papers as soon as you're ready."

"I... ah... I'm not quite ready for that. I want to look into a few more things."

"What things? Make a lowball offer and we'll send them the papers. I'm sure they'll take the deal."

Adam hated to broach the subject. He'd hoped to swoop in and out with the deal in hand and no complications, handle everything smoothly for his boss. A muscle twitched near his eye and beads of sweat broke out on his forehead. He sucked in yet another deep breath for courage. "Well, after meeting with the owner, I'm not sure she's going to be willing to sell. She seems pretty... attached... to the place."

"Did you talk to the young man? That generation usually likes the easy way out."

"I haven't yet, sir. I haven't directly approached the woman either."

"Well, get to it. I want the deal signed. I'm counting on you."

"Yes, sir. I will." Adam clicked off the call and stared aimlessly at the screensaver on his phone, a generic photo that had come with the phone he'd never bothered to change. He wasn't sure he'd even taken a photo he'd want to put as a screensaver. Who had time for photos and fancying up a phone?

His new boss's frustration with him was evident. He'd sent Adam down to Belle Island for one simple deal, and so far Adam hadn't even managed to make the offer, much less do any negotiations. He couldn't let his boss down.

He'd just have to toughen up and put his feelings aside. Act like the ruthless businessman he needed to be. He *needed* that bonus. He was going to get that bonus. Nothing was as important to him.

Not even the fact that he felt like a louse for hiding his real intentions from Susan.

That afternoon Adam went downstairs to meet Susan for their agreed upon walk to Lighthouse Point. He was wishing he hadn't set the date up yesterday. Not that it was a date. It was a walk. His mind spun. He had to pull it together and finish up his job.

Susan looked up from behind the reception desk and smiled at him. "There you are. Are you ready to go see Lighthouse Point?"

"I am." Well, he wasn't. But he also couldn't tell her that. He wanted nothing more than to talk to her son and feel him out, then make them an offer.

Susan turned to another woman at the desk. "I'll be back in a bit, Dorothy. Jamie is in the office if you need anything."

"Have fun." Dorothy smiled a warm look of friendliness.

Which just made him feel worse.

Susan came out from behind the desk and led the way out to the big deck that stretched across the back of the inn. A breeze blew gently in from the ocean and the sun rode high in the afternoon sky.

They walked to the water's edge and he fell into step beside her.

Susan strolled down the beach at an easy pace. "So have you heard our town legend about Lighthouse Point?"

"A legend? No, can't say that I have." He thought he'd researched almost everything about Belle Island.

"The legend says that if you make a wish and throw a shell in the ocean at Lighthouse Point, your wish will come true. Kind of like a wishing well, only it's…" Susan laughed. "It's a lighthouse and a shell."

"I see. Interesting tale. Have you made any wishes?"

Susan looked at him, her eyes sparkling mischievously, entrancing him in their spell. "I have, but I can't tell them. You know, in case that means they won't come true."

"Ah, good point." He wanted her to continue to look at him with her laughing blue eyes, but she perused the water's edge as they continued. They rounded the bend and the lighthouse came into view, standing over the island, protecting its shores.

"The sight of the lighthouse never fails to make my heart soar." Susan paused for a moment and he stopped beside her, taking in the view, then looking down at her.

Susan swept an arm wide. "I just love this island. Every single thing about it. I can't imagine living anywhere else. The island, the inn, working side by side with Jamie. I can't imagine a more perfect life."

A sinking feeling slithered down his spine. This island and running the inn were her life, and he was planning on doing his best to take that away from her.

Susan plopped down on the sand, and he sat beside her. She leaned back on her elbows and stretched out her legs, staring at the sea, lost in thought. He let his glance slide to watch her. The wind tossed her reddish-brown hair about, her cheeks had just a hint of a sun blush to them. Her nails were painted a delicate pink shade, and her only jewelry a simple watch and a leather bracelet. The faintest scent of orange and ginger floated around them.

She turned to him and caught him watching her. "Are you staring at me?"

He grinned guiltily. Guilt, it seemed like his constant companion these days. "Just a bit. You looked so relaxed and at peace."

"That's part of the magic of Lighthouse Point,

too. It's my special place. I come here to recharge, or unwind, or when I'm upset... or when I just need time to think."

"I can see why. The view is great. I imagine people have come and sat at this point for hundreds and hundreds of years."

"I know. I swear I can almost feel them when I'm here. Like the first woman who made the first wish. She was a Belle. Like the island, like Tally. It was a great-great some amount of greats grandmother to her. Her husband was lost at sea and she wished for him to come home. Legend says that six months to the day he came home and found her right here on Lighthouse Point."

"That's some romantic tale."

"It is. There are more stories, but that's how it all got started." She looked out to sea, then at him. "Well, we should probably head back. I told Jamie to take the evening off, so I better get going."

Adam stood and reached his hands down for Susan. She paused, then slipped her hands in his. He easily pulled her to her feet, and she swiped at the sand on her slacks. She took one last look at the lighthouse, then turned and headed down the shoreline. He fell into step beside her again, slowly walking along the edge of the ocean in the hard-packed sand. The waves slid up and splashed their feet and slipped back into the depths of the sea, mesmerizing him with each in-sync stride they took.

Adam walked silently beside Susan as they headed back towards the inn. He finally stopped when Susan paused and rested her hand on his arm.

"Adam, are you okay? You got really quiet." Her eyes were filled with concern.

And he felt like a jerk.

"I... yes, I'm sorry. I don't mean to be rude. I was just thinking work things. Going over them in my mind. Got a bit distracted. Sorry."

"No, that's okay. I know how work can get and how sometimes it seems to take over everything. I was beginning to worry that Tally and I talked you into walking out to the point, and maybe you just didn't know how to say... no." Her eyes held a tinge of self-doubt in their depths.

He looked down at her hand, still resting on his arm, the warmth of it spreading through him, connecting him to her.

Which was exactly the last thing he needed.

But her touch felt wonderful. It made him feel alive.

He promptly ignored the feelings.

"No, I enjoyed the walk very much." He wanted

to chase away the hint of insecurity in her eyes and assure her that he'd enjoyed his time with her.

He *had* enjoyed his time with her. Every single minute he spent with her his senses came alive and he wanted the moments to go on and on.

Things were not going exactly how he had planned. Not even close.

Susan noticed her hand still rested on Adam's arm and quickly snatched it away. She couldn't shake the feeling that something was wrong. His face held a troubled look and she'd felt he was a million miles away as they'd walked along the shoreline.

He smiled at her then, and his melancholy expression seemed to slip away. "I did have a good time. I like hearing you talk about the island." He grinned sheepishly. "I even considered tossing a shell into the ocean and making a wish."

"Well, you should have. There's powerful magic in that legend, hence the fact that so many places on the island have Magic or Wish or Luck in their name." She laughed and started back towards the inn. She sensed him right at her side, their arms almost touching, and at one point she was almost certain he was going to take her hand as they walked along.

And that would have been just fine with her.

Just fine.

Hm… maybe *she* should have made a wish while they were at Lighthouse Point.

CHAPTER 5

J amie entered the Lucky Duck, ready for a beer and a burger. Cindy was working late in Sarasota tonight and he hadn't seen his friend Harry in weeks, not since he and Cindy had gotten back from their honeymoon.

Harry waved from the end of the bar. Jamie crossed the battered floor and slipped onto the barstool beside his friend.

Willie, the bartender, walked up, a dishcloth over his shoulder and a bowl of nuts in his hand that he plopped down on the bar. "What can I get you?"

"Cold beer." Jamie turned to Harry. "You want another one? Sorry I kept you waiting."

"No, I'm good."

Willie brought a draft beer in a frosty mug and Jamie took a long-awaited sip. "That's what the day needed."

"Where's your pretty wife tonight?" Willie swung a tray of glasses to the counter behind the bar.

"She's working. I'm playing hooky for just a bit."

The door swung wide and two young women entered the bar, laughing. Willie grinned. "That's my cue. Going to go help those ladies out."

Harry laughed. "You do that, Willie. Wouldn't want them to get lost on their way to their table."

"Well, we wouldn't, would we?" Willie walked out from behind the bar and over to the women. One of them said something to Willie and he threw his head back and laughed uproariously.

"He's never going to change, is he?" Jamie asked.

"Doubt it. I don't think I've ever even seen him with a serious girlfriend. Well, not longer than a week or so." Harry took a swig of his beer. "But, that bachelor stage is way behind you now, buddy."

"It is, and you don't hear me complaining. I'm one lucky guy."

"You did all right for yourself, my friend," Harry agreed.

"Any prospects for you? I haven't even seen you date in forever."

"No one right now. Who has time for it? My business keeps me plenty busy."

Harry owned a real estate management company in town and Jamie had watched his friend grow the business. He managed rental property for many of the owners on the island. The business had flourished as his reputation for reliability had grown. "We've come a long way from the two kids running around the island and causing trouble, haven't we?"

"Speak for yourself. I caused trouble year round. I just got into more trouble when you came to town each summer." Harry grinned.

"So you're saying you were a bad influence on me, then?" Jamie cocked an eyebrow.

"Nah, we were just kids."

"At least we didn't get into any real trouble. My stepfather would have killed me." Jamie stared into his beer for a moment, lost in memories.

"At least he's not your stepfather anymore."

"No, he isn't. Glad to have the man out of my life and Mom's life."

"He was really something, wasn't he?"

His stepfather *had* been something. Now, even all these years later, he could hear the man's voice in his mind, telling him that he wouldn't amount to anything and that he'd always be a loser. No matter what Jamie had done, it was never enough to win his praise.

Jamie sighed. Why go down that memory lane again? He changed the subject. "So, tell me, how's business?"

"I got two new properties to manage this winter. I might need to hire someone else to help me."

"That's good though, right?"

"Yep."

"Well, if you run out of places for people to rent, you can always send them our way. Though, we are starting to fill up for the winter. Thanksgiving and Christmas weeks are full. January and February are almost full on the weekends. If we can just keep going and not have another big expenditure hit us, maybe we'll be able to turn the corner on this whole running the inn thing."

Harry raised his mug. "To success."

Jamie clinked his friend's mug and silently thought, from your toast to the fates' ears.

Julie walked into the beach house that her fiancé,

Reed, was renting. Her arms were laden with bags full of groceries. She was going to cook a fabulous dinner and then tell him she was ready to set their wedding date. She was tired of letting her fears hold her back.

That was just silly.

"Hi, sweetheart." Reed crossed over, swiped the bags from her, and set them on the counter. He turned and wrapped her in a hug. "I missed you."

"You saw me this morning when you stopped by The Sweet Shoppe."

"That was hours and hours ago. How is a man supposed to survive all that time without you?" He grinned and peeked in the bag. "Oh, pasta. Yum. You're spoiling me."

"Pasta and shrimp, and a salad. I brought a couple of slices of cherry pie, too."

"Well, if you're trying to win me over with your cooking, you do realize that you already have me, don't you?" Reed smiled the smile that warmed her and made her feel special, made her feel accepted and loved.

He helped her make dinner and they had their meal out on the deck. Afterwards he helped her clean up and do the dishes, then poured her a glass of wine. They went back out to the deck to watch the sunset. The whole time she had a running commentary in her mind telling her to just make the decision and pick a date.

She was going to tell him now. She was.

Right now.

"I have something to tell you, and I hope you'll be pleased." Reed's words broke through her thoughts.

"You do? What is it?" She looked over at him, admiring the golden light that somehow accentuated his innate goodness. She marveled once again at how lucky she was this smart, handsome, talented businessman was in love with her and she was nuts about him.

"Well, first, the bad news. I have to go back to Seattle for a few weeks to clear up some things."

She ignored the instantaneous wave of insecurity that swept over her.

"Don't look like that. You know I always come back." He took her hand. "I'm sorry it's so long this time, but I have meetings and things to deal with."

"When are you leaving?"

"Tomorrow morning."

"What's the good news, then?" She eyed him.

"Oh, that. I have kind of an early wedding present for you."

"But we don't even have a date yet."

"We will. I told you it was okay for you to take

your time. But, anyway, I decided... well... I bought this house."

"*This* beach house? But why? I mean, I thought you were renting it."

"I was, but Harry told me that the owner wanted to sell it so I scooped it up. You do like the house, don't you?" His forehead creased.

"I like it... it just seems like a sudden decision." And one he hadn't even consulted her on. Of course he wouldn't want to live permanently in her small cottage. He came from money and privilege, and she couldn't expect him to crowd into a tiny cottage. But she loved her cottage. It was all hers. She'd worked hard for it. For some reason, she hadn't even thought the whole living situation through. She'd avoided acknowledging that she'd have to leave her home.

Suddenly things started spinning out of control.

Reed looked at her closely. "Julie? You okay?"

"I..."

Reed moved over and knelt before her, taking both her hands in his. "I thought you'd like the surprise." He stared at her face, biting his lip. "I think I screwed up though. Maybe you would rather pick out a house together. I'm not good at this, Julie. I'm sorry."

"No, the house is wonderful. I like it. I just... Well, you surprised me."

"That's what surprises are supposed to do." He flashed her a wry grin. "But, I'm serious. I'll turn around and sell the place if you want me to."

"No, don't do that. You'll lose money."

"Money isn't important, you being happy is."

"I am happy. I *am*. Just give me some time to adjust." It seemed like she was always asking him to give her more time.

"I'll give you anything you ask for."

And the truth was, he probably *would* give her anything she asked for. She just didn't know what she wanted. His surprise decision had thrown a kink into her carefully prepared speech that she was ready to pick a wedding date. Because now? She wasn't so sure. Was he always going to be planning extravagant surprises? Would she become a part of his decision-making process on big decisions?

Reed settled back on his heels. "Well, I can see I have a lot to learn about this whole being engaged thing."

She leaned forward and pressed a quick kiss on his lips. "We both do."

CHAPTER 6

Late that evening Adam sat on the deck at the inn. The moonlight bathed the worn wooden planks dusted softly with sand. Everyone else had long gone inside, but the evening air was warm and the vast starlit sky unfurled above him. A peacefulness settled over him, and he allowed himself to forget his troubles and simply enjoy the moment.

"Am I disturbing you?"

He turned to see Susan standing beside him, and his heart leapt in his chest. "No, not at all."

"I... well, I brought out a couple of glasses of red wine... if you'd want one."

He took a glass from her hand, their fingers

brushing lightly at the exchange. "I'd love one. Will you come sit?"

She slipped into the chair beside him and propped her bare feet on the railing. "I love this time of night when most of the guests have gone to bed and the night is calm. There's just the sound of the waves on the shore."

"It is peaceful." He couldn't agree more.

"Well, sometimes it's still loud and noisy out here this time of night during the busy season or for a wedding or event. But when I can find a night like this I always try and come sit out here and just enjoy the moment."

The moonlight illuminated her face. She had that animated look that he'd grown to recognize when she talked about her inn.

Her inn. That was the problem. But he'd promised himself that he'd avoid his problems tonight, so he took a sip of his wine and propped his feet up beside hers.

"I can't imagine being able to walk out here anytime and enjoy the view or go strolling on the beach. It seems like such a... luxury... to me." Not that he took much time to sit and enjoy anything these days. His life was packed with work and responsibilities at home.

You're not supposed to be thinking about your problems, remember?

"It does feel like a blessing to be able to do this. I'm very lucky."

Her arm rested on the edge of the chair, and his was only a hair's breadth away from hers. He couldn't help himself, he reached over and covered her hand with his. She looked up, startled for a moment, then smiled.

She took a sip of her wine and leaned comfortably back in her chair. "So, where are you from? Where did you grow up?"

"I grew up in a small town in the Midwest. In Kansas. My mother still lives there." Kind of. His mother said she still lived there but he was fairly certain she'd never return.

"Where did you grow up?" He looked down at his hand covering hers.

"A lot of towns. My father was always getting a job, losing a job, getting a job. Mom would try and get a teaching job at each new town until it was time to move again. We lived all over the Midwest and parts of the Southeast, too. I think that's why I love being here so much. It feels like home to me. For the first time ever I truly feel like I belong."

Right now he could almost hear his mother's

voice scolding him for even thinking of blowing apart this woman's lovely life. Yet, that was his job.

You're doing such a great job with ignoring your problems. Such a great job.

He changed the subject. "So is it always such good weather this time of year?" Because weather was always a safe subject, right?

"Pretty much so. Fall here is just about perfect. Well, I do miss the colors of the leaves changing, but I don't miss the snow one little bit."

They sat for a while in silence, a comfortable silence, and finished their wine. Susan sighed and stood up. "I really should go in. I have a long day tomorrow. Well, every day is long." She smiled.

He got up and stood with her by the railing. He looked down at her and some crazy, overwhelming urge-thing overcame him.

"You know, Susan, I'd really like to kiss you right now."

Where was his off filter when he needed it?

Her eyes widened. "You would?"

"Yes, I really would."

A smile crept across her face. "Well, I think that might be just fine."

He leaned down and pressed a kiss to her lips. One of her arms came up and wrapped lightly around his neck. He pulled her tighter and deepened the kiss.

His senses finally came to him and he pulled away.

"Ah…" Susan stood there looking bemused.

"We should get you inside." He took her hand and led her back into the lobby, chastising himself every step of the way but knowing there was not one thing in the world that could have prevented him from kissing her tonight except a "no" from her.

CHAPTER 7

Adam woke up early the next morning and stood on the balcony sipping his coffee. His thoughts kept going back to the kiss last night. He shouldn't have done that. He'd let his feelings run away when he should have concentrated on being all business. But her sparkling eyes and soft voice had overcome him. Why, of all the women on the planet, was he attracted to Susan?

He saw Jamie head out to the beach and open the box containing the umbrellas and chairs. No time like the present to become the businessman he was supposed to be. He'd go talk to Jamie and get his thoughts on the inn before he came up with a firm offer for it. Adam knew he was running out of time. It was time to make the offer and see if he could close the deal.

He hurried downstairs and out to the beach. He crossed the cool sand. Jamie looked up and smiled as he approached. "Good morning."

"Morning. Looks like you have your hands full with setup today."

"During the busy season we have beach workers, but during the off-season I usually just do it myself."

"Your mother says you do a little bit of everything around here." Adam watched Jamie carefully to gauge his reaction.

"I do. Anything that needs to be done in the inn or the dining room. Repairs. Work on the books and do the taxes. I'm lucky that my uncle taught me so much about running the inn over the years."

"Do you enjoy it?"

"Well, it's hard work and long hours, but, yes, I guess I do enjoy it. I can't imagine doing something different. I've come to really love this inn. She's a part of me. I've been coming here since I was a small boy. Can't imagine life without it." Jamie's eyes lit up just like his mother's when he talked about the inn. "I get frustrated and overwhelmed sometimes, but on the whole, it's a great life. And

I'm helping provide financially for my mother. That's important to me. I want her to feel financially secure."

And just like that, Adam's hope of winning over Jamie on the idea of selling went up in a puff of smoke, dissipating across the waves in the breeze. There was no use delaying any more. He was going to go up to his room, get his papers in order, and set up a meeting with Susan and Jamie this afternoon.

His boss's voice reverberated in his mind. *Make sure you get it for the lowest possible figure.*

The problem with that? He no longer wanted to screw over either Susan or Jamie. He *wanted* them to get a very fair price for their inn.

To be honest, it was starting to bother him that his boss would probably rehab the inn into something unrecognizable from what it was now and had been for years. The character it had in every nook and cranny. Totally reworking the inn would break Susan's heart and probably break Jamie's, too.

Adam had a big problem with being the person who took that light out of Susan's eyes, even though he had no choice.

If he didn't make this deal and get the bonus, he didn't know what was going to happen to the one person he cared about most in this world—his mother. And there was nothing that would make him let his mother down again when she needed him.

In a strange twist of fate, what Jamie wanted for Susan and what Adam wanted for his mother were the same thing. The problem? Only one of them would get what they wanted.

～

"Well someone is in a good mood." Tally smiled as she walked into the office of the inn and heard Susan humming as she worked.

"Hi, Tally. I guess I *am* in a good mood." Susan grinned.

"Any particular reason?" Tally dropped into the chair across from Susan and watched while a faint blush crept across Susan's face.

"Ah, ha. It has to do with that Adam fella, doesn't it?"

Susan busied herself shuffling papers on the desk, then looked up sheepishly. "Maybe. I mean… yes."

"So that's all you're giving me?" Tally tilted her head to one side and gave Susan her best tell-me-everything look.

Susan sighed. "I… Adam kissed me last night."

"I figured he'd get around to it sooner or later. I

saw the way he was looking at you. Well, and the way you looked at him, for that matter."

"It seems a little silly though, doesn't it? I mean, he's only here for a few days." Susan pushed back from the desk, stood, and went over to the window. "But it sure was nice to have a man interested in me. It's been a very long time."

"Because you always walk away from anyone who shows the littlest bit of interest in you." Tally shot back.

"Well, I wasn't ready until now. But Adam is… different. He seems kind and honest."

"He's not hard on the eyes, either." Tally grinned.

"There is that." Susan tugged open the window, walked back to the desk, and sat down. "He's so easy to talk to. I like that. I never really had that with Russell. I did with Jamie's dad. I miss it. I know now I need that in a relationship. I need the friendship and companionship along with everything else."

"See, we learn things as we get older, don't we? And we don't settle for less than we need." Tally was glad that Susan had sorted this out and her friend knew what she wanted and needed.

"Well, I don't know where this is headed.

Probably nowhere. But I'll tell you one thing, I'm going to say yes if he asks me out again."

"As you should." Tally stood and walked to the door of the office. "It's good to see you happy like this."

"I *am* happy. My son is deliriously in love with his wife. I get to work with him at the inn—which is beginning to show a profit—kinda, anyway. And Adam is the first man who has caught my attention in a very long time… and he's an excellent kisser." Susan grinned. "Yes, I'd say that I'm happy. Life is just pretty great right now."

Tally found herself humming as she walked back in the warm sunshine to Magic Cafe. The salty sea air blew across her skin and she smiled to herself. Nothing like seeing a good friend happy to plop a magnificent mood right down on her, too.

Adam sat at the small table in his room and wrote up papers for a fair deal for Susan and Jamie. Not as low as his boss wanted, but he thought the man would still be in agreement. For some reason his boss wanted *this* property.

He stood and gathered his papers into a leather folder and walked out of the room to go find Susan and Jamie and see if he could talk to them. He headed down the stairs to the lobby, noting the elevator was still not working.

He walked up to the reception desk and a smile spread across Susan's face. She gave him the just-a-minute sign. He waited while Susan checked out a patron, coaxing an old printer to print a receipt.

Susan finished with the patron and turned to him. "Hi, can I help you with something?"

Her eyes sparkled, and the smile on her face blindsided him into numbness. He scrambled to put his thoughts together and get out his words.

Adam sucked in a deep breath. Now or never.

Just then the door opened and another person came into the lobby. He glanced over and froze. His boss stood in the open doorway.

He heard Susan gasp and turned to look at her. The color drained from her face and she grasped the edge of the reception desk. Adam looked at her, and concern swept through him. She looked like she was going to faint... or she'd seen a ghost.

His boss crossed the floor to the reception desk. "Susan."

"Russell, what are you doing here?" Susan voice emitted a frosty tone that Adam had never heard when she spoke.

"Business." His boss turned to him. "Did you get your job done?"

"Mr. Burns, I… um… I was just coming to talk to Susan."

"Talk to me about what?" Susan's eyes narrowed and a frown wrinkled her forehead. The color was rushing back to her face.

Just then Jamie came walking out of the office. He stopped and stared at Adam's boss. Adam noticed the same look of surprise that Susan's face had held. "What is he doing here?" Jamie walked up and stood protectively beside Susan.

"Well, Adam was to have dealt with all of this, but he didn't. So I came to see about the holdup."

"Adam is dealing with what, exactly?" Susan turned to search Adam's face, and he felt the blush of embarrassment flush his cheeks.

"Adam was supposed to make a deal to buy the inn."

"Buy the inn? We're not selling the inn." Jamie wrapped an arm around his mother's shoulders. "And even if we were, we'd never sell it to you." Jamie's eyes blazed with anger.

Adam realized he'd stepped in a mess of trouble he'd never seen coming. His boss had left out one *key piece* of information. What was Mr. Burn's relationship with Susan and Jamie?

CHAPTER 8

Susan fought to keep calm. The last person she'd ever expected to see standing in her inn was her ex-husband, Russell. Jamie radiated tension as he stood stalwartly by her side.

Susan swallowed, then glared at Russell. "Jamie is right. The inn isn't for sale."

"Don't be ridiculous. Everything is for sale for the right price. Besides I've seen the numbers. You're barely making ends meet."

"How would you know that?" Jamie's eyes glinted in anger.

"I have ways." Russell dismissed Jamie and turned to Susan. "I want this property. I have plans for it. I know you and Jamie don't have a head for business, so it was an easy decision to pick this place. After all, you two were always going on and on about the charm of this island. I don't see that, but I'm hoping the people who come to the resort that I'm going to build here will see it like you do."

Susan felt her mouth drop open in surprise. A resort here? Russell thought he could convert the inn into some kind of resort?

"Russell, we aren't selling the inn."

"You haven't even heard our offer." Russell's eyes narrowed in the way Susan remembered so well. The way they glared at her when he got annoyed with her, or when he acted like he wanted to swat her away like a bothersome gnat.

"It doesn't matter what the offer is." Jamie's voice was low and controlled. "We wouldn't sell it to you for any price."

"Don't be foolish, son." Russell glared at Jamie.

"I'm not your son." Jamie's voice held an edge of icy-cold fury.

Susan placed her hand on Jamie's arm. "Jamie's right. We wouldn't sell to you for any price. My dealings with you are over. Forever."

She glanced over at Adam, who was standing still as a statue, his face an unreadable mask, watching the conversation unfold.

She turned her attention back to Russell. "I think it best if you leave now."

"Don't be ridiculous. I'm offering you a way out of this hole you've dug for yourself. You two could move anywhere you wanted. Or stay on this godforsaken island. I don't care. Adam, make sure you leave the offer with them."

"No need, you have your answer. It's no." Jamie stepped out from behind the reception desk. "I'll walk you out."

Jamie stood toe to toe with Russell, and pride swept through Susan. Russell had done nothing but make Jamie's life miserable, and she was glad to see him stand up to the man.

"Well, we'll see about all this. I'll be back." The man turned on his heels and crossed the lobby.

"Don't bother." Jamie followed Russell to the door and closed it firmly behind him.

Susan took a deep breath and slowly turned to face Adam. A cascade of fury raced down her spine and she balled her hands into fists, clenching them tightly by her sides. "So all this was just you gathering information for Russell? You're in on this plan of his to take the inn away? It was all just part of your job?"

She felt like an old fool, thinking that Adam was interested in her. A rush of anger—or was it embarrassment—heated her cheeks. Of course he hadn't really been interested in her, he'd been pumping her for information. Any feelings she thought she had for him were promptly swept out to sea.

Adam started to speak, but she held up a hand and interrupted him. "No, don't bother. I think it best you go upstairs and pack your things. I'll check you out. No charge. Just leave."

Jamie came to stand by her side, his glance sweeping over Adam. "You're really something, Mr. Lyons. Coming here, pretending to be all nice and making friends with Mom. Anyway, you heard her. Go pack your things."

"I... didn't know..." Adam's eyes were filled with confusion and maybe a bit of regret. Not that Susan trusted her instincts anymore with this man.

"Ten minutes." Jamie stood by her side.

"Susan... I—" Adam reached out for her.

She held up her palms and stepped back. "Don't."

He looked at her for long, silent moments, then nodded and turned. She watched as he left the lobby before sagging against Jamie.

"You okay, Mom?" He wrapped an arm around her shoulder.

"I... just... I don't know."

"Why don't you head over to the cottage? I'll

make sure Adam leaves." Jamie's eyes filled with concern.

"I think I will. I don't want to see Adam again." She turned to leave, then spun back to Jamie. "Do you think Russell will go and leave us alone now?"

"I really don't know, Mom."

Jamie slammed around behind the reception desk, glad there were no customers in the lobby because he sure didn't feel like pasting on a friendly smile. He ripped open a ream of paper and loaded the printer. He dumped a handful of pens into the pen holder on the desk. He carefully aligned a stack of papers, then watched as they slipped to the floor. He bent over in exasperation, scooped them up, and plopped them behind the counter.

"Jamie, are you okay?"

He looked up to see his beautiful bride standing in front of the desk, a worried look on her face. "Yes." He raked his fingers through his hair. "I mean, no. I mean I don't know."

Cindy came around behind the desk and gave him a much-needed hug. "Talk to me."

"You'd never guess who was just here."

Cindy eyed him without offering up a guess.

"Russell."

Cindy stepped back, her eyes wide. "Really?" She frowned. "Why?"

"He wants to buy the inn." Jamie felt the anger rise up again.

"But, you're not planning on selling the inn, are you?" Cindy's forehead creased.

"No, of course not. And even if we were, we'd never consider selling to Russell. Not after he screwed over Mom in the divorce. Not after all the years he treated me like… well, like he wished I'd never come into his life."

"I'm sorry, Jamie." Cindy wrapped her arms around him and held him tight. The faint scent of lavender enveloped him, calming him.

"Where's Susan? Is she okay?"

"I sent her over to the cottage for a bit." Jamie pulled out of the embrace and sighed. "And you know that guy I told you about that I thought Mom was interested in?"

"That Adam guy?"

"That one. It appears he was just here to scope out the place and see what kind of lowball deal he thought they could offer for the inn."

"Oh, Jamie. Your mom must be crushed."

"Crushed, mad, hurt—you name it."

Jamie looked up to see Adam walk across the lobby and approach the desk, carrying his suitcase.

Adam put his room key on the counter along with a folder. "Here is our offer."

"You needn't bother. We're not going to sell to Russell."

Adam looked Jamie directly in the eyes. "I had no idea Mr. Burns knew you two. None at all. I just knew he wanted this property."

"He more than knows us. He was married to my mother, he was my stepfather."

A look of surprise swept across Adam's face. "He... what?"

Jamie almost believed Adam's surprised look was genuine. But then, since he didn't trust the guy, there was no reason to believe him now. "Russell was married to my mother. For years. He divorced her and left her with absolutely nothing. Now it appears he's coming after even more. But it won't happen. This inn is her whole life now. She loves it. I'm going to make this inn so successful it will make Russell's head spin. I want that for my mother." He wanted that for *himself*.

"I'm sorry. I had no idea about any of this. No idea of his connection to you. I'm sorry."

"Well, sorry doesn't cut it. You came here, asked Mom out, became friends... all of it was a lie. You hurt her. Don't expect me to forget that." Jamie heard the icy threat in his voice.

Adam stood silently for a moment then nodded. "No, I don't expect that you will."

Adam turned and walked out of the door. Jamie spun around to Cindy and wrapped his arm around her. "Heck of an afternoon," he whispered against her neck.

She held him tightly and he once again thanked his lucky stars, or his wish at Lighthouse Point, or the fates, for giving him the chance to spend his life with this woman.

Adam slowly walked down the steps of the inn out into the blinding sunlight and crossed over to his car. He squinted in the bright light and retrieved his sunglasses from atop his head. He turned and took one more long look at the inn, uncertain how he'd gotten in the middle of this mess and why Mr. Burns hadn't told him about his connection with Susan and Jamie. None of it made sense.

Well, he knew his boss was ruthless in business. It appeared he was ruthless in his personal life, too. Or maybe, he just thought the inn was a great deal and couldn't care less if, in the process, he hurt people who used to be family. Or maybe, like Jamie had said, Mr. Burns was coming after more.

Adam was certain he'd never forget the look on Susan's face when she called him out for not telling her the real purpose of his trip. He hadn't really meant to trick her, he'd just wanted to figure out the right way to approach Susan and Jamie. But all that had backfired.

His boss was mad that the deal wasn't closed, Susan was hurt, Jamie was furious with him… But how was he supposed to choose between Susan and Jamie… and his mother. And if he didn't fix this, it looked like once again he was going to let his mother down when she needed him most.

He looked at his phone and saw an incoming text from Mr. Burns.

Reservation at the Hamilton Hotel in Sarasota. Meet you there.

His chaotic roller coaster of emotions mocked him. The brief time he'd been able to spend with Susan—and he'd enjoyed every single minute of it —well, that was over. He'd ruined that along with crushing her trust in him.

He slid into his car and muttered under his breath, "Heck of an afternoon."

CHAPTER 9

Susan had given into tears last night, after Russell and Adam had left, but this morning she was more mad than anything else. Late morning she headed down the beach to Magic Cafe. The fresh salty air did little to sooth her jangled nerves. She climbed the steps to the restaurant and slipped into a chair across from Tally and Julie.

"You okay?" Tally's face held concern. "All Jamie said when he called me was that Russell came to town and I should see if we could meet."

"Jamie worries about me too much." Susan reached out for the offered coffee cup, savoring the rich aroma. "But I am glad to see you two. I feel like screaming. I will never get that man out of my life."

"What happened?" Julie leaned forward, concern etched on her face.

"Russell came to town. He… he wants to buy the inn."

"But it's not for sale." Tally frowned. "Why does he want it?"

"Jamie had Harry do some checking around. It looks like Russell has bought the property beside the inn, along with a large property across the street."

"I don't get it." Julie frowned.

"I think he's trying to buy up a large swath of property and… well, open some kind of resort."

"You think he wants to rehab the inn?"

"I guess. Then add to it? I'm not sure. I don't know why he picked *this* area when there are a million other places he could buy." Susan sipped her coffee and carefully set the cup back down. "I guess we spoke too highly of the area. I never thought he listened when we'd come back all excited from one of our trips here. He rarely joined us on our visits to Belle Island and he really doesn't have anything good to say about the island now. Well, except that he wants to buy the inn. But it's always just business with Russell."

"I'm sorry, that must have been such a shock." Tally scowled.

"Well, that's not all. You know Adam?"

"The guy you're trying to act like you're not interested in?" Tally asked.

"Yep, that guy. The one who kissed me."

"What?" Julie sat up straight.

"Yes. He did. But, for the record, I'm so not interested in him. At all. At least now." Susan looked out at the ocean, then back at her friends. "Well, he was in on it. He was just trying to get information about the inn and see what problems we're having. He was trying to figure out what kind of offer to make. They did leave an offer... it is just... well, Harry looked at it for us and said it was below market by quite a bit. Though, what kind of market is there for an inn? I don't know. It's not like a ton of people are looking to buy one. Anyway, I don't want to sell it."

"Of course you don't. You've come so far with it. Each year you get closer to turning the corner on making it really profitable," Julie agreed with her.

"And it's Jamie's whole life." Susan paused and traced a track of water on the table top. "But, sometimes I wonder if it's what he really wants. What if we could get money for the inn and he could go and do anything that he wanted? He just kind of fell into running the inn."

"Jamie loves the inn as much as you do." Tally

scooted her chair back from the table and stretched her legs. "You both love it. Don't let Russell make you doubt yourself."

"You're right. Russell does have a way of making me doubt every decision I've ever made. I shouldn't let him have that power over me." Susan turned to her friends. "Enough of this. I sent Russell away. Adam is gone. Life goes on, but remind me to choose more carefully if I ever consider thinking I might like a guy again. Anyway, things will calm down and get back to normal. Now, what's new with you two?"

Julie hadn't ever heard Susan talk about a man she was interested in, much less one she'd kissed. She could tell her friend just wanted to move onto a new subject. Well, she had a story to share.

"I have some news." Julie tossed a tiny smile. "Reed got me a wedding present."

"He did? Does that mean you set a wedding date?" Susan's eyes sparkled with hope. "We're all set to have it at the inn if you want."

"No, not exactly. I was going to tell him that we should set a date, but then he surprised me with the present."

"What was it?" Tally cocked her head to the side.

"He bought that beach house he's renting and deeded it to me."

"No kidding." Tally looked thoughtful.

"I know I should be grateful, he's always so generous. But it was such a big decision about where we will live and—well this might sound silly —I didn't even get a say in the matter."

"That's not silly at all." Susan reached over and touched Julie's hand. "Of course you'd want to be consulted on a big decision like that. No one likes someone else to take control of her life."

"He did apologize to me after he saw my reaction. I guess I wasn't excited enough. To be honest, part of it just hit me so hard. I'll have to give up my cottage. I mean, I can't ask him to move into my tiny place. He's used to living in really nice homes. But that cottage means so much to me. My first real house. I'm afraid any other place won't really feel like my home. I told you I'm just having silly thoughts, aren't I?"

"No. You're acknowledging how you truly feel. That's not silly at all." Tally scooted her chair up and leaned on the table. "You've worked hard at getting The Sweet Shoppe profitable and buying your first ever home. You should be proud of that. I think what you should do is sit down with Reed and really talk to him about how you feel. I know you're used to keeping things bottled up inside to protect yourself, but you're not that scared little girl anymore. You need to stand up for yourself. Tell Reed what you need."

Julie sighed. "I tried to tell him, but I was just so shocked."

"Then you need to try harder." Tally pinned her with a listen-to-me stare.

"You should listen to Tally. She gives good advice." Susan lips lifted into a gentle smile.

"I know you're right. I will talk to him when he gets back from Seattle. Hopefully we'll sort everything out and I will set a wedding date. I will." She would, wouldn't she? Something seemed to be holding her back and she wasn't quite sure what it was. Was it really that she didn't want to give up the cottage? And if that was it, how selfish was that? Reed had given up so much for her. He'd even moved to Belle Island and worked remotely. She needed to sort this all out.

Tally watched her friends head down the beach, arm in arm, going back to the inn and The Sweet

Shoppe. She was worried about both of them. Susan had looked devastated about that Adam character. Tally would love to give him a piece of her mind if she ever saw him again. And that Russell had some nerve trying to swoop in and take the inn from Susan. What would Susan and Jamie do without the inn? It meant everything to them.

And as long as she was thinking about clueless men, what was Reed thinking when he bought the beach house without talking to Julie. Didn't he know her better than that? Didn't he realize she was taking baby steps to adjusting to being engaged and trusting that he would be there for her?

Maybe he thought buying the place would be a grand gesture to prove he was here to stay. Anyway, Julie needed to talk to him and sort it out. Reed was a good man, he'd listen and understand.

Tally sighed. This was the reason she never dated anymore. It just complicated your life. She'd had her chance with love and romance. That was all in her distant past. She had her friends and Magic Cafe. Her life was good. It was.

Tally turned to clean up their table. The cafe would be opening for lunch soon and she still had a long list of to dos before it opened.

She gathered the dishes in a gray tub and carried them to the pass-through to the kitchen.

KAY CORRELL

She went and unlocked the door to the cafe and welcomed her first customers. As she sat them outside, she heard someone call her name. Her friend Paul and his new wife, Josephine, waved from across the restaurant.

She motioned for them to come sit down. They crossed the distance, with Paul carefully leading Josephine with a light hand on her elbow.

"Tally, so good to see you." Josephine smiled as Paul held out the chair for her.

"It's good to see you two, too. It's been a while."

"We were up in Mississippi visiting my sister. She's living in my old house in Bay St. Louis and we also saw my niece and nephew in Comfort Crossing." Josephine reached for the offered menu.

"We had a nice visit, but it's good to be home." Paul settled into the chair across from Josephine.

Josephine smiled at Paul. "Belle Island is starting to feel like home to me these days, too."

"That's what we like to hear." Tally watched the couple as they settled in and started sipping their coffee. The smiles they sent each other were like a magnetic connection. A connection that affected no one else in the universe. Paul deserved that.

She and Paul had been friends for years. He'd helped her with business advice when she struggled with opening Magic Cafe. She'd given him her full

76

support when he opened his art gallery on the island. She was happy Paul had reconnected with the love of his life. She'd never seen him so happy and content. It was obvious that Josephine adored him, too. A picture perfect happy couple.

It appeared that some people *were* able to find never ending happiness on Belle Island.

CHAPTER 10

Adam finished up lunch with Mr. Burns. His boss had been only too explicit in his demands on closing the deal on the inn. Adam assured him that he would continue to work on it and had given Jamie their offer.

"I'm counting on you, Adam. I'm not willing to go much higher than that original offer. They should stop being so ridiculous. They should be happy to get out from under the debt. Jamie always did think with his emotions instead of his head. Susan isn't much better. They don't have a lick of business sense between the two of them." Mr. Burns slapped his leather folder shut. "You'll take care of this?"

"I'll do my best, sir."

Mr. Burns got up and strode out of the restaurant at the Hamilton Hotel. The man always walked as though he owned the place, no matter where he was. His boss disappeared around the corner, leaving Adam to finish his coffee and ponder his fate. He wasn't sure Mr. Burns was right. From what he had seen, he thought that Susan and Jamie had made a lot of smart business decisions regarding the inn. He just wasn't sure this was a deal that Mr. Burns was going to win.

But, of course, that left Adam in a very bad place. Not only would he lose out on the bonus, he was pretty sure he'd lose his job. Then what in the world was he going to do? It had taken him months to find this job. It's not like jobs just grew on trees. He knew how to evaluate commercial property such as the inn. He knew how to turn them profitable. He knew how to negotiate a deal. But, if he lost this job, he'd not only be out his salary, he'd be out the bonus and he needed that desperately.

He looked up from his thoughts to see the woman he'd seen with Jamie yesterday standing beside the table. "Mr. Lyons."

"Hello. I saw you at the inn yesterday, didn't I?"

"Yes, you did. I'm Cindy, Jamie's wife. I'm here at the hotel heading up the rehab of the Hamilton."

"I heard he'd just recently married."

"You and Russell are staying at the Hamilton?"

"We are. I hope that's not a problem."

"No. Better here than at the inn." The woman paused and looked directly at him. "Susan is really hurt, you know. Not that she'd show it. It was a rotten thing to do."

"I assure you I had no idea Mr. Burns was her ex-husband and I was not trying to just get information. I enjoyed her company." He sighed. Enjoyed it more than he had with any other woman in a long, long time. "At first I was trying to figure out the best way to approach Susan and Jamie, I admit that. But Susan is... remarkable."

Cindy's eyes widened then narrowed as she frowned. "So, you're going to drop the whole buying the inn thing?"

"I'm afraid not. Mr. Burns is set on having the property."

"I heard he's bought up property around the inn, too."

Adam wasn't surprised Susan had already figured that out, so there was no use denying it. "He has."

"So he has plans to expand the inn? Make some kind of resort?"

"Yes, a resort." Adam was torn between blurting out the fact that Mr. Burns would most likely redo the inn into a resort that was barely recognizable as the old inn. It wasn't his fact to tell. He had his job. A job he wished more than anything was no longer his to do. Of course, he might get that wish, because Mr. Burns might fire him.

But he couldn't let that happen.

"Well, you might as well tell your boss that there is no way Jamie and Susan will sell to him. There is too much history, none of it good. I'm pretty sure they'd rather the bank take it back than Russell."

"But then he'd just buy it from the bank and the end result would be the same, but they wouldn't get any money for it."

Cindy chewed her lip and looked thoughtful. "Well, they are in no danger of the bank repossessing the inn these days."

And Adam was glad of that, even if it meant he was going to fail.

Cindy sat in a back office at the Hamilton Hotel. Her desk was spread with swatches of material and carpeting samples. Mr. Hamilton was in a hurry to get things ordered for the renovation. He'd bought the old Magnolia Hotel in Sarasota and wanted to update everything, inside and out. At times the project alternated between thrilling her and overwhelming her. But she kept her planner with her always with sections on all the details to make sure nothing fell through the cracks.

"Cindy."

She looked up to see Mr. Hamilton standing in the doorway. Darn it, she always liked to make sure her office was picked up when she knew he was coming to town. "Mr. Hamilton, I didn't expect you."

"Camille decided she wanted to come for a few days' visit to Belle Island, so I came along to check on things here at the hotel."

"Things are going well. I'll have the final choices for you to confirm in just a few days. Now that I know you are here in town, I'll have them ready for you before you leave if you'd like."

Mr. Hamilton nodded. "That would be great. The photos you sent can only do so much. I do like everything you've planned for the hotel so far."

"I know, you said understated elegance. I'm hoping I hit that note for you."

"So far you have. I know my father prefers a darker, more opulent style, but I'm hoping that this new rehab will be successful for this hotel. If so, hopefully we'll be able to update a few of our older properties."

"I'm excited to see it all come together." Cindy knew it would be a long process and the biggest job she'd ever done, but she was confident she could make it work. Pretty confident, anyway.

"Delbert, honey, I've been waiting forever for you. Are you about finished?" Mr. Hamilton's girlfriend, Camille, entered the office.

"I'll be right with you. We're just finishing up."

Camille walked over, stared at the swatches on the desk, and frowned. "You're going to go with that color range?" She turned to Mr. Hamilton. "Delbert, your father won't be pleased. He likes rich, dark colors."

"I'm trying to do something different. A bit more modern, still elegant, but a bit lighter in color. I think Cindy has done a great job so far."

Camille's face held a definite I-doubt-it look. "Well, I'm going to the lobby. Don't keep me waiting much longer." She let out a long-suffering sigh. "I knew I should have insisted you drive me to the island first."

Mr. Hamilton shot an apologetic look at Cindy. "I think your options you've been showing me are great. I look forward to seeing the final choices this week. We need to discuss new furniture for the lobby, too. I'm also thinking we need all new poolside furniture, nicer furniture and I'm thinking of adding a poolside bar."

Cindy grabbed her planner and scribbled notes as her boss was talking.

"Well, I should go. I don't want to keep Camille waiting any longer. I'll be back later this week without her and we'll sit down and make some decisions." He turned and hurried out the door.

Cindy sat at her desk, overflowing with the piles of samples, and wondered how she was going to make her final selections to show Mr. Hamilton in just a few days. She'd thought she would have at least a few more weeks to make decisions and collect estimates. She was going to have to put in some long hours. She picked up her cell phone to call Jamie and tell him she'd be home late tonight.

CHAPTER 11

A dam drove over to Belle Island again that evening. For some reason the island lured him like a siren. He knew better than to go to the inn, so he parked his car in town and went to take a walk on the beach. He figured he'd watch the sunset and try to sort things out. He'd already stayed longer than he planned, and he didn't have many more days that he could be away from home.

Everything had turned into a colossal mess, most of it his fault, both here and back in Atlanta.

He found himself walking towards the lighthouse and decided that was as good a destination as any other. He trudged down the beach, his feet sinking into the sand. He crossed to the hard-packed sand and continued around the bend until the lighthouse came into view. He walked up near it and stared out to the sea. Maybe he should make a wish like that crazy island legend encouraged.

He looked both directions and didn't see anyone who would witness his lack of sanity. He leaned down and picked up a shell that seemed to call his name. He turned it over in his palm, then squeezed his hand tight.

"I wish... I wish I could have a do-over and make this right for everyone."

He tossed the shell out in the sea and sank to sit on the sand, watching the sky begin to burst into brilliant colors.

A lone beach walker came from the other side of the lighthouse, looking mostly out at the sunset along the way. As the person got closer—before it was really possible to tell—Adam knew, *he was certain*, it was Susan.

He stood and brushed the sand from his slacks. If fate was going to practically drop Susan in his lap, he was going to run with it. Adam knew he had to make another attempt to explain himself. He didn't want her to think that his only reason for going out with her was to find out information about the inn. He was worried about her. He'd seen the look on her face when she'd seen Russell, and then Cindy had so bluntly confirmed he'd hurt Susan.

He watched her approach and knew the exact moment Susan recognized him.

Susan stopped in her tracks. What was Adam doing back on the island? She thought she'd made it perfectly clear he needed to leave. Why was he here? The last person she had expected to see on her walk this evening was Adam, right here at Lighthouse Point. Her heart fluttered, a traitor to her feelings because she was *not* happy to see him. She wasn't. There wasn't a tiny thrill running up her spine at the sight of him, there couldn't be.

She was an old fool. The man was nothing but a liar.

There was no place to run, no place to hide. But then why should she run? Why should she hide? It was *her* island. *He* needed to leave, not her.

She stalked up to him. "I thought you'd left."

"I did. I came back."

"You have no reason to be here. We're not selling. Go back home. Leave us alone. You tricked me. I can't forgive that."

"Susan, please. Just let me talk to you. Give me five minutes. Please."

Adam's face wrinkled, entreating her to give him a chance. She stared at him, then nodded, saying nothing more to the man.

A look of relief swept across Adam's face. "First off, I had no idea that Mr. Burns was your ex-husband. I don't know why he didn't tell me, but he didn't. You have to believe me."

No, she didn't have to believe anything he said, even if he did look sincere. But then, what kind of judge of character was she, anyway? She'd certainly judged him wrong, thinking he was actually interested in her. She remained silent.

"At first I hung around you because I wanted to figure out the best way to broach the subject of selling the inn. I admit that." He paused and sighed. "Not proud of that, but it's the truth. But as I spent more time with you, then I... well, I know it sounds crazy because we just met, but I started to care about you. Your life and Jamie's. That kiss? It meant something to me."

Susan was not going to let him see the kiss had meant something to her as well. She'd never admit that. Besides, she still wasn't sure she believed him. The butterflies in her stomach mocked her, taunting her as if to say the kiss did mean something and she'd felt something she hadn't felt in years and years.

"My boss promised me a bonus if I get this contract negotiated and finished. I… well, I really need that bonus, not to mention I need this job. The way he talked when he turned the task over to me, I thought it was almost a done deal and that you'd want to sell. I just wanted to get the best price for Mr. Burns and impress him."

"So, it's all just about money to you?"

He looked at her, a trace of pain flickering across his face. "No, it's not just about the money, but I assure you, I really do need that bonus now, or I'd walk away from all of this."

Well, that was honest. He said it like it really was. He'd walk away from her except for the money.

"Well, you had your five minutes. I heard everything you said. We're not selling so I guess you won't be getting your bonus." She walked past him then turned back for a moment. "Goodbye, Adam. Tell Russell to leave us alone. I don't want to see you again, either."

"I *am* sorry, Susan." A look of sadness hovered over his expression. She could almost believe him. Almost.

She turned around and started walking. She didn't want to hear any more of his excuses.

CHAPTER 12

The next morning Susan woke up and stretched like a lazy cat. For a brief moment she couldn't remember where she was, then everything came back to her. She was staying at the inn to give Jamie and Cindy privacy, and Russell was a jerk, and she never wanted to see Adam again. That about summed up her life right now in one lightning strike of comprehension.

She got up, dressed, and headed downstairs. Might as well start her day. There certainly was enough work to keep everyone busy.

She entered the kitchen and saw the cook standing by the stove. Just standing.

That was a problem.

The cook should have already had things started by now.

"There you are, Susan. I've tried everything, but this stove is not going to come on no matter what I do. We have the old stove—well, the *really* old stove — as opposed to this *old* stove, but I won't be able to keep up with all the orders with just the one."

"I'll put a notice in the menus that it's just a continental breakfast today. I'll call Julie and see if I can pick up more baked goods. We'll have cereal, yogurt, granola, fruit and pastries." Susan sighed. "I'll have Jamie call Harry and see if he can fix the stove. He can fix just about anything. We don't want to be buying a new stove now."

Susan left the kitchen to type an insert for the menus and a sign to place at the receptionist stand letting their guests know there was only a light breakfast available today. At least they could heat up the bakery items in the oven… if that didn't give out on her, too.

She called Julie, who answered on the first ring. "Julie, I need your help."

Of course Julie agreed when she heard Susan's predicament. "Sure, I can help you out. I'll bring some extra over on my delivery and have Nancy start baking some more for the shop. It won't be a problem. We haven't been that busy."

"I really appreciate it."

"It's not a problem, really. I'll see you in just a bit."

Susan clicked off the phone, printed up a paper that would do for a menu today—offering a twenty percent discount to their guests for the trouble—and went into the dining room to explain to the hostess what was happening.

By the time she got back to the kitchen, Julie, laden with baked goods, was walking in the back door. Susan hurried over and took a tray from her, then walked out to the van to bring in more items.

"Thank you, you really saved me this morning." Susan looked at the trays of muffins, danish, and cinnamon rolls on the counter. "I don't know what we'll do about dinner. Might have to close if we can't get the stove working."

"I'm sorry." Julie gave her a hug. "It's always something, isn't it? Like you need this on top of Russell's shenanigans yesterday."

Susan accepted her friend's hug gratefully. This hadn't been her best week. "Thanks for the bailout."

"Listen, I gotta run. Let me know if I can do anything else to help." Julie turned and slipped out the back door.

Jamie entered the kitchen. "What's this I hear about the stove?"

"The cook can't get it to work."

"I'll call Harry and see if he can drop by. I know we need to replace at least one of these old stoves with a new one, but it keeps getting pushed down the list. I'm thinking now is the time to get a new one. I guess we'll shut down the restaurant until we can get one in if Harry can't coax this one back to life. But either way, I think we should order a new one."

"I'm afraid you're right. There goes the money we had set aside to paint the outside this year."

"Ah, let's just say the weathered look adds to the inn's charm." Jamie grinned.

Susan laughed. "Okay, we'll go with that bit of marketing until we can scare up more money for the painting."

"I'll go call Harry."

"Thanks, son." Susan watched Jamie walk away and looked around the kitchen. More than just the stove needed replacing, but they'd been getting by okay.

Getting by just fine, right?

"Thanks, Harry." Jamie walked his friend out of the kitchen. "I guess we'll have to order that new stove."

"Well, I have it working for now, but, honestly, it's not going to last much longer. I rewired it, but I make no guarantees."

"I'll be looking at new stoves today."

"Sorry I don't have better news."

"No, I just appreciate your help, as always." Jamie smiled at his friend. "Ever wish you weren't the handiest guy that everyone in town knows?"

Harry laughed. "Nah, I don't mind fixing things. Glad to help out. You owe me a beer for this one, though."

"Okay, next time Cindy works late and I can get away, I'll give you a call."

"You know, you're welcome to actually bring Cindy out with us. I'm thinking she's here to stay." Harry's face crinkled into a big grin.

"Okay, we'll set something up."

Jamie walked back to his office and sat at the computer. He pulled up a few sites and looked at prices on new stoves. It wasn't pretty.

What if Russell was right? It seemed like they were always just one repair away from disaster. His uncle hadn't kept up with repairs and updates in his later years of running the inn. They were constantly playing catch-up now.

Jamie gritted his teeth. There was no way—*no way*—that Russell was going to be right. Jamie opened their bookkeeping program and looked at the numbers.

That wasn't a pretty sight either. He got up and walked to the window, staring at the gathering storm clouds. He did not want to fail his mother. He'd find a way to make this work.

CHAPTER 13

J amie headed to the mainland to visit the restaurant supply store and check out new stoves. His mom had left him to pick out a new one, but he wasn't ready to make a decision. He wanted to talk to someone in person about their needs and figure out which one to order. It always made him second guess himself when they had major purchases at the inn.

He left the supply store more confused than when he'd been looking online. Or maybe he just hated spending the money. They had just replaced the hot water system that had finally given up on them this summer. Now the stove. All the carefully saved money was swirling away in a constant stream of repairs.

He decided to stop in at the Hamilton Hotel to see Cindy. Maybe she'd even have time for lunch. He pulled into a parking space and strode into the hotel lobby. The hotel that Delbert Hamilton had bought to rehab and make into one of the Hamilton Hotels was an older boutique hotel. Cindy said the hotel had great potential. They were planning on keeping it open while they did the renovations, then having a grand opening of it when it was ready to officially become a Hamilton Hotel.

He texted Cindy as he walked into the lobby. Within a minute she came hurrying out to the lobby and gave him a quick hug. "This is a nice surprise." She smiled at him then looked at him closely. "But something is wrong, isn't it? I can tell."

"Just repairs and replacements at the inn. The stove is dying just like the hot water system died. There are so many old things at the inn that need to be updated."

"I'm sorry." Cindy's face filled with concern.

He kissed her quickly. "It's okay. I'll figure it out. Anyway, do you have time for lunch before I head back to the island?"

"I have a bit of time. Let's just grab something here in the restaurant. Is that okay?"

"That sounds perfect." No better way to boost his spirits than spending time with his bride.

They walked into the restaurant and got a table. They ordered, but Cindy got called away. "I'll be back in just a few minutes, I promise."

"No, go ahead. I'm fine. I know you're busy."

"Just a few minutes." She leaned over, kissed him, and hurried out of the restaurant. He watched her walk away, still a bit in shock at his good fortune that she was his wife.

Adam strode into the restaurant with a file of papers under his arm. He'd only had coffee for breakfast and his rumbling stomach reminded him it was time to eat. He'd have himself a working lunch. He looked over and saw Jamie sitting at a table by himself. Without thinking, Adam threaded his way over to Jamie's table.

"Hello." Adam stood in the aisle.

Jamie looked up in surprise, then his eyes narrowed. "What are you doing here? Following me?"

"No." Adam gave a wry smile. "Mr. Burns and I are staying here at the Hamilton. Listen, Jamie, I want to apologize to you. I tried apologizing to your mother, but... well, she wasn't having it. I don't blame her. But I assure you I had no idea that Mr. Burns was your stepfather."

Jamie sat stony faced.

"I didn't mean for your mother to get hurt. That was the last thing I wanted."

"Was it?" Jamie tilted his head. "I'd think the last thing you wanted was to not be able to get the hotel for Russell."

"Okay, I deserve that, but I like your mother. I like her a lot. She's charming, and funny, and I enjoy her company. The time I spent with her... well, it's the best time I've had in a long, long time."

"She's hurt." Jamie's eyes glistened with a piercing glare.

"I know that, and I can't apologize enough."

"No, you can't." Jamie stared at him. "What is it you want? You already know our answer."

"I just wanted to say I'm sorry how it all went down."

Jamie searched Adam's face. "Maybe you're sorry, but it really doesn't change things. My mother loves that inn. She works hard. I want more than anything in the world to make the inn a success. For her. To prove Russell wrong. For me. But mostly for my mother. She deserves that and so much more."

Adam felt an immediate kinship to the young man, a bonding, because truth be told he felt the exact same way about his mother. She deserved so much better than life had dealt her, and he'd do anything to make her life better.

It didn't help his already piled-on guilt that Jamie was just trying to do the same thing for Susan, that he was trying to do for his own mother. To give her what she needed. Jamie was a good son and Adam admired his fierce protectiveness of Susan.

Adam had a sinking feeling that he was never going to close this deal, never get the bonus he needed, and he'd hurt someone he'd come to care about in the process. Oh, and let's not forget he'd let his mother down, too, when she needed him most.

Susan bit her lip as she paced back and forth in the office. Why was the county inspector here? They weren't due for another inspection for quite a while. Had someone turned in a complaint?

The man was taking his own sweet time looking over everything. He'd already been in the kitchen… thank goodness they'd gotten the stove working.

He'd noted that the elevator wasn't working now. Bad timing. Unfortunately, one of their handicap accessible rooms was on the top floor. Susan had made sure they had one rehabbed room with a view that was handicapped accessible. But, of course, it wasn't handicapped accessible if the elevator wasn't working. Which meant it probably put them under the required number of handicapped rooms. It hadn't been a problem because they hadn't had two handicapped rooms requested at the same time when the elevator was out... but that probably wasn't going to make a difference to the inspector.

Jamie walked into the office. "Hi, Mom." He stopped and looked at her. "What's wrong now?"

"Oh, Jamie, the inspector is here."

"That's not good. We're trying hard to make sure we're up to code... but why is he here again anyway? He was just here a few months ago. We passed everything."

"I don't know and that worries me. Do you think we had a complaint?"

"Well, none that we've heard about." Jamie frowned.

Susan paced back across the office. "I wish he'd just finish up and give us his preliminary findings."

"Excuse me." The inspector stood in the doorway.

Susan pasted on a welcoming smile. "Hello, I hope you found everything fine just like you did a few months ago. Was there a problem? Is that why you're back?"

"A hotel is always subject to inspection. We try to do surprise visits every so often to just check on things." The man held out a piece of paper. "You have quite a few violations now."

Susan took the paper and had to stifle a gasp. The paper held a long, long list of items. She looked at the man. "You found nothing just a few months ago."

"Must have missed a few then." The man shifted from foot to foot and looked down at the ground.

Jamie took the paper from her. "Are you joking? Look at some of these things."

"Well, they'll need to be fixed. I understand the non-working elevator is a common occurrence. I'm going to suggest that you be required to rehab another first floor room to be handicapped accessible, along with fixing those items."

"What?"

"There are laws, ma'am. You need a certain percentage of your guest rooms designated handicapped. With an undependable elevator, I'm afraid we can't count your upstairs room."

"Of course not." Jamie rolled his eyes, and

Susan didn't miss the heavy sarcasm dripping from each word.

"We're going to have to downgrade your rating on the restaurant, too, until these items are fixed. I'll send the written report and be back to check on the changes." The man turned and left.

Susan frowned. "That whole visit was strange. We never have more than minor write-ups. Look at some of these. They are costly to do." Susan sank onto her chair, frustrated.

Jamie scowled. "You don't think Russell had something to do with this, do you?"

Susan looked at her son in surprise. "I don't know. He wouldn't do that, would he?" She thought back on hearing all the discussions at the business dinners she'd held when she was married to Russell. The men did laugh about ruthless moves they made in their dealings.

Susan set the page on the desk and turned to Jamie. "I'm afraid you might be right. Russell might stop at nothing if he wants the inn badly enough."

"The guy is a heartless jerk. Always has been. Always will be," Jamie growled the words. "Well, he's not going to win this time. I'm so over the man. We'll figure something out, Mom, I promise."

She only hoped her son was right.

CHAPTER 14

Adam tapped his phone to answer the incoming call. "Hi, Mom."

"Adam, I thought you were only going to be gone a few days." His mother's voice sounded concerned.

"I was. I'm sorry. Things got… complicated. It's taking longer than I thought."

"I just wanted to be sure you're okay."

"I'm fine, Mom." He should have called her more regularly, just one more thing he'd messed up this week. He'd only talked to her once since he'd gotten to Belle Island. "I think it will still be a few more days."

"Okay, son. You do what you need to do. I'm

fine here. I just wanted to check and make sure everything was okay with you."

He should be checking on *her*, not her checking on *him*. She sounded fine, but he'd feel better if he spoke with her caretaker. "Can I talk to Martha?"

"She ran to the grocery store. I'm sure she'll be back soon."

Adam knew that Martha wouldn't have left for long. He'd been lucky to get her to stay with his mother while he was out of town. Usually Martha just came by for an hour or so each day to check on his mother while he was at work. "Okay, I'll call her later and check in."

"Okay, I'll see you soon."

"Bye, Mom. Love you."

The phone went dead and he sank into the chair in the corner of his room. He set the phone on the table and sunk his head into his hands. His mother deserved so much better and he was going to make sure she got it.

But was he going to have to destroy Susan and Jamie's life in order to give his mother the life she deserved?

Jamie set the table while Cindy finished making the

meal. It had been days since they'd actually both been able to sit down for dinner together.

"Can you pour us some wine?" Cindy turned from the stove.

"Yep, sure will." Jamie poured two glasses and set them on the table. Cindy had added a pretty tablecloth and matching placemats. She always had some pretty flowers or other centerpiece on the table, too. She liked things arranged and neat. He and his mother had always just eaten on the bare table, and even then it was a rare occurrence. He had to admit he'd eaten standing up at the sink more times than he cared to admit. At least the window over the sink had a view of the ocean...

Cindy sat across from him and passed him the shrimp risotto she'd made. "Here you go. Hope you like it. I do love that we can get so much fresh fish here. I'm learning more recipes using seafood."

Jamie took a bite. "This is really good."

Cindy beamed. "Glad you like it."

Jamie was pretty sure he could spend the rest of his life like this and be the luckiest man alive. A wife he loved, a job he enjoyed, and quiet evenings like this.

Cindy took a sip of her wine. "So you ran into Adam at the Hamilton?"

"I did. He kept apologizing, but that doesn't really fix it, does it?"

"I really think he's telling the truth. He actually seems like a nice man."

"For a nice man, he certainly is causing enough problems." Jamie set down his fork. "And now we have more problems. The inspector came today and gave us a long list of things to fix."

"Really?"

"Really. And he downgraded the restaurant until he comes back and sees the fixes. We've never had a list like this. Plus, you know Mom, she keeps the kitchen spotless and is always on everyone for safe handling of food and keeping it clean. She was shocked."

"I'm sorry."

"I'm wondering if Russell is behind all this." It certainly wouldn't surprise Jamie to find out his stepfather had a hand in the surprise inspection.

"Would he do that?" Cindy frowned.

"In a heartbeat. Russell does anything to get what he wants. Plus, the inspector was just here a bit ago. This is really close for another visit."

"What are you going to do?"

"Fix every darn thing on the list and call him back to re-inspect. Though, if Russell is behind it, I'm not sure the guy won't just find more problems." Jamie sighed. "Mom is really stressed now."

"She works really hard."

"She does." A stab of guilt hit Jamie. "She works hard, long hours, day in and day out. I sometimes wonder if she does it just for me. So I can have the inn."

"Oh, Jamie, I think she loves the inn, too."

"You're right, I think she does. But it's a hard, busy life." Jamie turned and took Cindy's hand. "I wonder if we should take the offer. She'd have money. She could do what she wanted. Buy a small house on the island. Work part time or an easier job without endless hours.

Jamie let go of Cindy's hand and took a sip of his wine, his mind whirling with conflicting emotions and thoughts. "I sometimes worry that maybe she's keeping it because of me."

"I don't know. I really think she loves running the inn with you." Cindy squeezed his hand. "You're always doing what you think is best for your mother. One of the many things I love about you." She leaned over and kissed him. "I know you'll do what you think is right… but I'm afraid it will destroy you to sell this place to your stepfather."

Ex-stepfather, as if that made any difference now. Jamie leaned back in his chair. Cindy was right. It would kill him to sell the inn to Russell... once again proving Russell's stance that Jamie was a failure and couldn't make a success out of anything.

Adam met Russell in the lobby of the hotel the next morning. He'd thought that Russell would head right back to Atlanta, but so far no such luck. The man was probably watching to see what Adam could do with the deal.

"So did you contact Susan again? Now that she's had time to calm down—always thought she overreacted—did she realize what a good thing it was to take my offer? Maybe the offer was too high. Bet I could have gotten it for even less money now." Mr. Burns laughed. "I did pad our odds just a bit."

"What are you talking about?" Adam looked directly at his boss.

"Let's just say that a few well-placed dollars will get an inspector to do a really, *really* thorough job on inspecting the inn. I hear they got quite a list of things that didn't pass, money that will need to be spent... oh, and wouldn't you know? Their restaurant got downgraded, too." Mr. Burns shook his head with a Cheshire cat grin plastered on his face.

"You…" Adam didn't even know how to say it. "You paid someone to inspect the inn and fail it? To write up bogus violations?"

"No, of course not. I just made a little investment and requested a *thorough* inspection of the inn. I did not say to fail things." The grin sat on Mr. Burns face like a badge of success.

Adam knew his boss was a tough businessman, he just hadn't realized how far he'd go. He frowned but then quickly hid his displeasure.

Mr. Burns pointed a finger at Adam. "So, I want you to go over and tell them they have one day to decide if they want to take my offer, and it's only good for another twenty-four hours. If we have to make another offer, it will be lower. Got that? I'm thinking I just made your job easier for you."

There was not a thing about this job that was easy.

"I'm headed back to Atlanta today. I want you to close the deal. Your bonus depends on it." Mr. Burns looked Adam straight in the eye. "Close the deal by the end of the week, or it's over. You're out. Don't let me down."

Mr. Burns spun around and walked away while Adam allowed himself a minute of panic.

And then another one.

CHAPTER 15

Adam knew he had to go to the inn and tell Susan about Mr. Burns' new twenty-four hour deadline. He wasn't sure how his boss could justify a lower offer after that window, because this one was pretty bottom of the market already.

But then if the inspector was causing problems and running up expenses for Susan to fix the problems, well Susan and Jamie were going to be between a rock and a hard place with nowhere to turn.

And he, Adam, was the instigator of all their problems. Well, that's not right, he rationalized. Mr. Burns had already decided he wanted to buy the inn before Adam had been hired. Though, part of the reason he'd been hired was his tough negotiations on other hotel buyout deals.

Right now he wished that he had any other skill in the world. Why hadn't he become a dentist or an accountant or something? At least he wouldn't be hurting Susan now.

He slowly walked out to his car, barely noticing the bright sunshine and warm weather. A dark, rainy day would have suited him better. He didn't even know how he'd get Susan to listen to him long enough to give her the new edict of twenty-four hours.

He drove meticulously under the speed limit, in no hurry to actually get to the island. He felt like a kid heading to the principal's office, knowing what was in store for him when he got there.

He pulled his car into the parking lot of the inn. He slipped out of the car and stood looking at the old building. It had a lot of character in a well-loved way. It had a few quirky add-on wings and one corner had a rounded turret that ran three stories high, giving those rooms a nice three sided view. The inside had most of the original woodwork. He hoped Mr. Burns planned on keeping the majority of these things intact. They were part of what gave the inn its charm, but he was sure his boss planned on updating everything.

He took a deep breath and headed into the inn. His eyes adjusted slowly to the darkness inside. He headed over to the door to Susan's office.

Susan came rushing out and ran smack into him. He reached out his arms to steady her. She leaned against him for the briefest moment and he felt a surge of protectiveness race through him.

As soon as she was steady, she glanced up at him and jerked away, rubbing her arms where his hands had just been. "Why are you here? Haven't you done enough? Hasn't Russell done enough? I know he was behind the inspector visit, so don't even try to deny it."

"He was." The heat of embarrassment crossed Adam's face. "I didn't know he was going to do that."

"Well, that does me no good now, does it? You didn't know he was my ex. You didn't know he was sending the inspector. You don't know much, do you?" Her words held an icy edge.

"I... ah, no." He stumbled for words. "I am sorry for your troubles."

"Right."

He didn't miss the big dose of sarcasm.

A sick feeling deep in the pit of his stomach swelled through him. "Well, you're going to be even angrier with me, but Mr. Burns has said to tell you the offer we made stands for twenty-four more hours. After that, the next offer will be lower."

Susan looked at him in disbelief, then a look of sadness swept over her face.

He wanted the floor to swallow him whole. He wanted to take back his words. He wanted to be working at any other job in the universe right now.

Susan looked at Adam, so disappointed in the man she'd thought she might like. Even just a little. Right now her feelings bordered on extreme dislike leaning towards hate, but she didn't truly hate anyone.

Except maybe Russell.

"You delivered your message. Our answer is still the same. We won't be selling to Russell."

Susan watched while the blush of embarrassment covered Adam's features. Good. He should be embarrassed. The original offer had been a joke. Going lower wouldn't even cover what they owed on the property. One too many loans for improvements to the inn. Now, just when things were looking up, Russell had started causing trouble.

"So, you're leaving?" Susan stood her ground.

118

"I will." Adam reached out and placed his hand on her arm. She jerked her arm away.

"I'm sorry." Adam's eyes glistened with sincerity.

She didn't really doubt he was sorry. But it was probably sorry the deal wouldn't go through, not the mess that Russell was bringing to her life. She turned away.

Once again she felt his hand on her arm. She paused.

"Please, listen to me," Adam implored. "I am sorry you're going through this. The job is important for me because... well, I have my reasons. Good reasons."

She turned to look at him, his hand still searing a brand on her bare skin.

His eyes pleaded with her to understand. "I... well, it will make a difference in the life of someone I care about."

Susan waited for more of an explanation.

"It's important, I swear, or I'd walk away from all of this."

She eyed him skeptically.

"I truly, truly am sorry." Adam let go of her arm, spun around and walked out of the lobby.

There was no doubt in her mind that Adam really was torn on this business deal and something very important to him was riding on the success of closing the deal. She'd seen the raw emotions on his face, the pain in his eyes. He couldn't fake that. Instinct told her his emotions were very real.

The thing was… it wasn't going to happen. She wasn't going to sell to Russell. She stood lost and adrift on a sea of conflicting emotions.

CHAPTER 16

Cindy walked into her office at the Hamilton to find Camille riffling through the papers and samples on her desk.

"Excuse me?" Cindy approached the desk and Camille looked up in surprise. "Why are you going through my things?"

"I…" Camille stood up tall and did an obvious regroup. "They aren't exactly *your* things, now are they? You work for Delbert. I'm sure he wouldn't mind me looking at what you were planning on suggesting to him."

Cindy bit her tongue, holding back the stream of words she wanted to let loose. She looked at the mess of samples on her desk. The samples that had been neatly piled into her first, second, and third choices.

Camille tossed her hair back over one shoulder. "You have no right to question me. I'm sure Delbert will listen to my opinion, and all of these samples are just so wrong for this hotel. It needs to be... well, classy. Grand. These are just... well, all wrong."

"I think they are just what Mr. Hamilton wants for the hotel." Cindy grew a backbone and held her ground, which kind of surprised her. Up until recently she would have been the first one to give in and make peace. But this—*this*—was *her* project.

Camille's eyes widened. "You're not questioning my opinion are you? I know what Delbert wants."

"What do I want?" Mr. Hamilton came walking into the office.

Camille spun around. "Delbert, honey, I was just giving Cindy here some advice. Some of her choices seem so... simple. Not what one would expect in a Hamilton Hotel."

Mr. Hamilton crossed over to the desk and looked at the now messy pile of samples.

"Mr. Hamilton, the samples are all..." Cindy shot a glance at Camille. "They are a bit jumbled together now. I'll get them sorted out with what goes with what." If he looked at that mess on her desk he'd think she didn't know what in the world she was doing.

Her boss looked at Camille, then back to Cindy. She could see him take a deep breath then turned to Camille. "Camille, dear, I think you should let Cindy do the job I hired her for. So far I have been impressed with all her work."

"But Delbert—"

"No, I'm serious, Camille. I would appreciate if you would…" Mr. Hamilton took an obvious deep breath. "I'd appreciate it if you could just let Cindy do her job without interfering."

"Well, I never." Camille's face blushed a bright red. "You think she has better taste than *I* do?"

"I didn't say that. I simply think she understands the look I want for this hotel." Mr. Hamilton smiled at Camille, trying to placate her.

"Fine. Ruin the reputation of your father's hotels. Do that. Just don't expect me to stand by and watch it."

"Camille, you're being a bit dramatic. You know I care about you and care what you think. I just want Cindy to have free rein to come up with ideas without being influenced by what has always been done. I want this to be a new flagship hotel, a new look." Mr. Hamilton's eyes shone when he talked about the possibilities for this hotel.

"If what Cindy thinks is more important than what I think, well, then I'm just going to leave. I'm going to head back to Comfort Crossing and visit Mama. This is just… *not* what I expected from you, Delbert."

"Camille, darlin', don't be like that."

"Our trip to Belle Island is over. I'm leaving today."

Mr. Hamilton sighed. "As you wish, but I need to stay here and finish up some business. I'll see you back in Comfort Crossing in a few days."

"Maybe. Maybe you need to do some serious thinking about your priorities. I won't be treated as less than…" Camille turned to Cindy. "As less than a mere *employee*."

Camille spun around and flounced out of the office. Cindy stood silently trying to process her thoughts on the whirlwind that she now thought of as hurricane Camille.

Mr. Hamilton turned to Cindy with a wry smile. "Camille leans a bit towards the dramatic. I'm sorry."

"Ah, no, that's okay." Camille picked up a sample and set it carefully on the edge of her desk, wondering how long it would take her to sort everything back how she'd had things.

"I am fond of her. She's her own worst enemy."

Mr. Hamilton shrugged. "Fortunately, or unfortunately, I find myself truly caring about her, so I just deal with her… episodes. She has a kind heart, she just doesn't show it very often."

If he said so.

Cindy didn't believe it for a moment. She thought the man was just a bit besotted with Camille. Everything she had heard about and seen with Camille leaned toward her being a self-centered diva.

"Anyway, don't let Camille's comments throw you off. I'll be back in a few days and we'll make the final decisions. So far I've been impressed."

"Thank you." A wave of relief swept through Cindy. She was a bit annoyed that she'd let Camille's comments about how she wasn't making good decisions get under her skin. She thought once she'd learned to stand up to her mother and sister, standing up to other people who tried to make her decisions or belittle her would be easier. But the tiny bit of the old always-compliant-don't-make-waves Cindy sometimes would break through her new resolve.

She watched Mr. Hamilton walk out the door and looked down at the mess that Camille had made of her desk. She reached down and picked up a piece of paper that had fallen to the floor. It had

Camille's name written on one side. She turned it over and froze in place.

It was a past due notice from the largest ritzy department store in the South. The amount that was past due boggled Cindy's senses. Her first car had cost less than Camille's bill.

She slowly folded the paper, wondering what she should do with it. She didn't feel like she could give it to Mr. Hamilton to give to Camille, but Camille had said she was leaving town. She could find out Camille's address in Comfort Crossing, but then Camille would know she'd seen the past due bill.

She set the paper on her desk, still unsure of what she was supposed to do with it.

The computer screen was taunting and mocking Susan again. What had she ever done to it? She looked at it in disbelief. Five new reviews on the Florida Travel website. Each one a bad review. There was no way this was a coincidence, any more than the inspector's visit had been. Russell was trying to sabotage the business.

She tried to remember why in the heck she'd ever

married the man. Oh, he'd been charming at first. He'd treated her well, showered her with presents. Though, now that she looked back on it, it was always presents that he could show off to his friends and business associates, not necessarily something she would actually want. A fancy diamond bracelet, a brand new car, a trip to some exotic location with other business friends of Russell's.

Then, it was like he'd lost interest in her. She was expected to play hostess at dinner parties, but the fancy jewelry gifts stopped and he started going on the business trips without her.

She should have seen it coming, but she'd stuck with him year after year, until he'd had his lawyer deliver a merciless divorce agreement.

So, it wasn't like she didn't know the man was ruthless, she just wasn't expecting him to turn that heartlessness on her once again and try to take her inn away from her.

She looked up at the sound of someone coming into the office.

"Mom, you okay?" Jamie's forehead was creased with worry.

"We have five new reviews on the travel website. All bad."

"What? We rarely get a bad review and five in a

row?" Jamie walked over and peered over her shoulder.

"That's got be Russell's doing."

"I'm sure it is. But the thing is, we can't prove it, so the reviews will stay out there."

Jamie let out a huff of air. "He's really intent on ruining us in hopes we'll sell to him."

"Well, there's more."

"I'm afraid to ask…"

"Adam was by here yesterday afternoon and said the offer was only good for twenty-four hours. The next offer will be lower."

"That Adam is a peach of a guy." Jamie rolled his eyes.

Susan didn't know why she felt a sudden urge to defend Adam. "I honestly think he's sorry about all the trouble this is causing us. He said he had reasons why he needed this deal to go through."

"Yeah, like lining his pockets with a bonus."

"I don't know, Jamie. I got the feeling he was really feeling torn."

Jamie looked at her closely. "Mom, you don't still have feelings for the guy, do you? After all he's done?"

"No… I just… I think he was sincere with his apology yesterday."

"Like that helps anything." Jamie sighed.

"Mom, please don't let him sucker you in again. He's bad news."

"Don't worry. I have my eyes wide open now."

Jamie turned to leave and Susan sat staring at the computer screen. As if to mock her troubles, the computer abruptly shut down.

Just one more problem in a long list of problems.

Susan got up and walked out of the office. Dorothy came over to her and said in a low voice, "The fire marshal is here."

Adam stared at the report Mr. Burns had just sent him. His boss hadn't mentioned one *tiny little detail* to him about the project.

Mr. Burns intended to tear down the inn.

Completely.

That would devastate Susan.

Adam dropped the report onto the desk in his hotel room and paced the floor. Mr. Burns had originally said they planned on incorporating the inn into the resort plans. By incorporate it appears that the only part of the inn they planned on keeping was the land...

He let out a long whoosh of air and snatched

his car keys from the desk. He had to get out of here and think.

Before long, Adam found himself back at Lighthouse Point. It was as if that small part of Belle Island had a magnet that drew him back. Or maybe it was because he had come here with Susan and had such a wonderful time. He'd only known her a short time, but he'd instantly felt comfortable with her.

Well, until he'd blown her world apart.

He stood at the edge of the sea and watched a pelican swoop down into the water and back up with his meal, just like Russell swooping down to take away Susan's livelihood.

Adam was torn in two directions. His responsibility was to his family, to his mother, but everything Russell was doing to Susan was wrong.

He swooped down just like the pelican and grabbed a shell. "I wish I didn't have to make this decision between Susan and my mother." He threw the shell as far as he could into the ocean.

I wonder if there's a limit of wishes you could make at Lighthouse Point.

He sank onto the warm sand and dug his heels in, making shallow troughs on the beach. He picked up another shell and ran his finger along the edge worn smooth by ages of tumbling in the waves.

"Adam."

He looked up in surprise to see Susan standing above him. He sprang to his feet. "Susan, hi. I was just… thinking."

"It's a good spot for that. I figured a brisk walk might help me stomp off my anger."

"Did it?" From the look on her face he was pretty sure the walk hadn't helped much.

"Nope. We had an unexpected visit from the fire marshal. It wasn't good. Two citations. It's not like I don't want the inn to be safe. I do."

"I'm sure you do."

"It wasn't even the regular inspector. It was someone filling in for him. Our fire extinguishers in the kitchen expired yesterday. Jamie actually has it on his list to buy new ones tomorrow when he goes into Sarasota. Their expiration date is written on the yearly report, so I don't think it's a coincidence we were inspected one day after their expiration date. And, of course, they still work. He also found one malfunctioning smoke detector in the middle of one hallway. The regular inspector would have pointed that out and said he'd come back in a few days to make sure the corrections were done. This guy? He wrote us up."

Adam didn't know what to say to all this. It sounded suspiciously like Mr. Burns' work.

"Oh, and let's not forget the bad reviews up on the travel website." Her eyes flashed with righteous indignation.

"Susan, I want to say that I didn't know, but I'm always saying that to you. The fact is I should have known he would keep trying anything and everything to sway you into taking his offer. He's probably not finished, either."

"Probably not." Susan's voice didn't sound quite defeated, but she did sound tired.

He looked out at the sea with its slowly rolling waves, then glanced at the lighthouse as if for moral support.

Suddenly, his decision was made.

He turned to Susan. "I'm going to quit my job."

"You're what?" Susan looked at him in surprise.

"I just don't want to work for a company, for a man, who does his business like this. It's not right."

"You're going to quit over this?" Susan cocked her head to one side and eyed him with doubt.

"I am. I'm going to call him as soon as I get back to the hotel."

"I thought you said you had important reasons that this job needed to work out."

"I did. Well, I *do*." He raked his fingers through his hair. "But it's just not worth it. I'll find another way."

How was he going to find another way? He had no leads on another job, this one had been hard enough to find. But there was no way he could live with himself if he continued on helping Mr. Burns destroy Susan's life.

He reached out and took Susan's hand. "I'm sorry for any part I played in this. Let me make it up to you. Let's see if we can find a way to make Mr. Burns go away and find a different piece of property."

"You'd help us save the inn?"

"I would. I've done some tough negotiations on business deals. I should be able to put that to good use. We need to try and stay a step ahead of Mr. Burns or find another way to thwart him." Adam felt at peace with this part of his decision at least. "I need to settle some things first, but then we'll see if we can figure a way out of the mess I got you into."

Susan squeezed his hand. "It wasn't really you who got us into this mess."

"Well, I played a big part."

"How about no more apologies, no more I'm-sorrys? And we would love to have your help and any ideas you have to throw Russell off his dog-with-a-bone grip on wanting the inn."

"I have to leave for a day and check on… things. But I'll be back. I promise." He didn't miss the look of doubt in her eyes. He wanted to kiss her and chase those doubts away, but he held back. He didn't think she was ready for a kiss and she probably didn't trust him yet. But he was going to make it up to her. He was.

"I'll be back the day after tomorrow. I promise."

CHAPTER 17

Adam went straight from the Atlanta airport to his office the next morning, gathered up a few of his personal items, and put them in a neat stack. He looked around the modern, magazine photo-spread worthy office and thought of it in contrast to the inn, with its cranky computer, friendly workers, and personable ambience. He liked the cramped office at the inn better than this cold, impersonal, gleaming one.

He took the elevator to the top floor and told Mr. Burn's secretary he needed a moment with his boss. A few minutes later she ushered him into his boss's office. The corner office had a view of the Atlanta skyline and was decorated with the best of everything, right down to the best bourbon on the well-appointed bar at the side of the room.

"Adam, I hope you come with a signed contract."

Adam looked down at the paper in his hands. "Actually, I come with a signed resignation."

Mr. Burns jumped up from his desk and planted his hands on the desktop, his eyes flashing. "What nonsense is that?"

Adam took the few steps to the desk and placed the single page on the desk. "I quit. I can't be the one to take that inn away from Susan and Jamie, and I certainly can't be the one to do it with underhanded tricks. I've had enough."

"You're making a big mistake." Mr. Burns spit the words at him.

"No, I don't think so. I'm making the best decision for everyone." He only hoped it was true.

"Well, I don't accept your resignation. I'm firing you."

Adam sniffled a wry grin.

"And furthermore, I'll make sure you don't work anywhere in Atlanta again. Or anywhere in the state. Or with anyone I have the remotest connection to. You'll get no recommendation from me, obviously." Mr. Burns stood red-faced, leaning across the desk. "I can ruin you if I want."

"Well, sir, you can try. But I'll still have my integrity." With that, Adam spun on his heels and left Mr. Burns' office. His pulse thundered in his temples and his momentary sense of doing the right thing warred with a crushing panic.

"Mom, you here?" Adam dropped his suitcase inside the front door of his mother's apartment. The apartment that was right down the hall from his.

"Back here, honey."

Adam walked to the sunroom where his mother loved to sit. Sunshine streamed through the window as she sat in her favorite chair, working on a crossword puzzle. She did a lot of puzzles these days, saying they helped to keep her mind active. He leaned down and kissed her cheek. "Everything going okay?"

"I'm fine. I wish you'd quit fussing over me."

She did look fine, but he never knew when she'd have a bad day. She'd gotten lost once, but a stranger who he'd be forever grateful to stopped when he saw her looking confused and called Adam from the emergency contact on her phone.

"Where is Martha?"

"She left. I told her you were coming home today."

"She was supposed to stay until I got here." Adam knew his mother was alone some, but he didn't like it to be for very long. He worried she'd leave something on the stove to burn, or who knew what. He constantly worried about her, even though he was pointedly reminded by her that she didn't want him hovering.

"Adam, you were gone longer than you said. She did us a favor to come over the extra days."

His mother was right, he owed Martha a great deal. She was always willing to help out. Now he needed to call Martha and see if she could stay over while he went back to Belle Island to fix this mess he made.

His mother looked up from her crossword. "Anyway, Martha was headed out of town today to go visit her grandchildren. I told her to get an early start before the traffic picks up."

His heart sank. The only person that he'd carefully vetted to take care of his mother was out of town. Now what could he do? He'd promised Susan he'd come back and help her.

He looked at his mother, her gray-haired head bent back over her crossword puzzle, pen in hand. There was no way he was leaving her alone.

"Hey, Mom, how do you feel about taking a little trip with me?"

CHAPTER 18

J ulie entered her small cottage at the end of a long day. She'd been staying at her house instead of at Reed's bigger beach house while he was out of town. It felt more like home to her. She threw her purse on a chair, slipped out of her shoes, and padded into the kitchen to pour herself a glass of wine. She wanted to go up to the widow's walk and sit and unwind.

She started up the stairs with her glass in hand, but paused when she heard a knock at her door. She turned around, a bit annoyed for the interruption.

She tugged the door open. "Reed." She threw herself into his arms. He hugged her tightly.

"I thought you were going to be gone for another week or so."

"I came back for a few days. I missed you."

Julie smiled and pressed her cheek against his chest. His strong heartbeat thudded against her ear. He held her for another moment or two before releasing her.

"So, what have you been up to while I was gone?"

"I was just going to take a glass of wine up to the widow's walk. Want to join me?"

"Sounds good. I could do with some unwinding."

They went up to the widow's walk and sat in the chairs on the walkway. Julie took a sip of her wine and looked over at the man she had fallen hopelessly in love with. Tally was right. She just needed to talk to him and tell him how she felt.

She sucked in a breath of courage. "Reed, can we talk?"

"Sure, what's up?" He turned to look at her.

"I... well, you kind of blindsided me with buying your beach house without talking to me. I know you meant it as a wedding surprise, but I felt kind of... left out... left out of making a big decision like where we were going to live. I'm afraid you're always going to make decisions like that without talking to me. I know I've struggled to have control over my life, and it just... all of a sudden I lost control over where I'll live."

Reed's face twisted into a frown. "I'm sorry. I realized when I told you about it and saw your face that I had screwed up. We can sell it. That's not a problem."

She took another deep breath. "And part of it was that it made me realize I'll lose this cottage. And I love this house. I bought it and it's the first place that's ever been all my own. It will be so hard to leave. I know it's small and too cramped for both of us to live here. You're used to living in really nice homes. I know that."

Reed leaned over and took her hand in his strong one. "Don't you know that I'd live anywhere with you? If this house makes you happy, we can live here. I'm fine with that. Honest. And we can sell the beach house, I'm fine with that, too. And I promise I'll never make another big decision like that without talking it over with you."

She looked him straight in the eyes, her heart overflowing with love for this man. "Well, how about we make a joint decision on a wedding date. I'm ready to set the date now."

"Really?" Reed's eyes flickered with happiness, and he snatched his phone out of his pocket. He pulled up the calendar app and grinned. "Well, look at that. It looks like I have absolutely any day free that you pick."

CHAPTER 19

"So Adam quit his job with Russell? Because of us?" Jamie stood at the other side of the desk, staring at his mom in surprise.

Susan nodded. "He said he couldn't work for a man like Russell. He left to go back to Atlanta and turn in his notice. He said he'd be back today, but I'm not sure he meant it."

"Why is he coming back here?" Jamie wasn't sure he liked the news that Adam was returning to Belle Island.

"He said he was coming back to help us find a way to stop Russell from interfering with us. He feels responsible for our troubles, though it's not really his fault."

"Well, he certainly didn't help matters any."

Jamie scowled. "I think he should just stay in Atlanta and leave us alone."

"I'm sorry you feel that way."

Jamie spun around to find Adam standing right behind him in the entrance to the office.

"I… ah." Jamie felt the heat of embarrassment flush his face.

His mother jumped up and crossed over to Adam. "You came back."

"I said I would."

Jamie didn't miss the sparks flying between Adam and his mom. Adam took his mother's hand in his and for a moment Jamie thought the man was going to *kiss* his mother.

"We're going to find a way to stop Russell and fix the damage he's caused." Adam's gaze hadn't left Susan.

His mother seemed to have forgotten Jamie was in the room, too. It was like only the two of them existed for a brief moment.

"I have someone I'd like you to meet." Adam's face held a tentative look.

"Of course." His mother's gaze still hadn't left Adam.

Adam led his mother out of the office and Jamie trailed behind them, not quite willing to let his mother out of his sight in Adam's company. He still didn't trust the man.

~

Susan followed Adam out into the lobby. He walked up to an attractive older woman standing in the lobby looking a bit lost. "Mom, I want you to meet Susan."

The woman smiled and reached out to take Susan's hand. "Adam has told me all about you and your son. I'm sorry for your troubles. I'm sure Adam will be able to help you."

"Nice to meet you Mrs. Lyons." Susan smiled back at the woman.

"Oh, please, call me Mary."

"Mary it is." Susan looked at the woman who had Adam's same sky blue eyes. Or, she guessed it was really that Adam had his mother's eyes.

"So, I guess we'll need two rooms, if it's okay that we stay here?" Adam looked at Susan.

"Of course it is." Susan led them over to the reception desk. "Dorothy, do we have two rooms side by side, or how about the suite, is that empty?"

She turned to Adam. "The suite is two rooms with a sitting room in-between."

"Ah, I... we'll just take two rooms. Going to watch expenses until I find another job."

Jamie walked up. "Dorothy, give them the suite. No charge."

Susan was surprised at Jamie's offer. She hadn't missed that her son was none too pleased that Adam had returned.

"I couldn't." Adam shook his head.

"Yes, you can. You're here to help us. We're not charging you for your room." Susan stepped forward. "Dorothy, you remember Adam. And this is his mother, Mary."

"Nice to meet you, Mary. Glad to have you here with us." Dorothy coaxed the computer into putting in the reservation for Adam and Mary.

"That's very nice of you to give us the suite. Thank you." Mary smiled at Susan. "Maybe I could help out with things around the inn while you and Adam work on thwarting that Mr. Burns fellow?"

Susan didn't miss the flash of concern that crossed Adam's face.

"Oh, you don't have to help while you're here. You can just have a little vacation."

Mary patted a tote bag she was carrying. "Well, except for my knitting and my crosswords, I have a lot of free time."

"Oh, you're a knitter and crossword

person?" Dorothy's eyes lit up. "My two favorite pastimes. I'd love to see your knitting project. And there is a wonderful yarn shop on the island. We could go there and pet the yarn…" Dorothy laughed. "I mean buy some yarn."

Mary's eyes shown. "I'd love that. I used to have a knitting group I'd go to, but then I moved to a new place in Atlanta to be near Adam."

"We have a knitting group that meets tomorrow. You could come with me."

"I'd love to."

Dorothy reached out and gave Adam two keys. "Here you go."

"Let me show you the way to your suite." Susan waited while Adam picked up his suitcase and his mother's. She led them to the corner suite at the far end of the inn on the first floor.

Adam and Mary entered the room.

"Oh, it's so lovely." Mary looked around the sitting room then crossed over to the French doors that led to a small patio. "Oh, Adam, come look at the view. It's so pretty."

"Told you it was a special place, Mom. I knew you'd love it."

"Well, I'll let you two get settled." Susan turned to leave.

Adam walked her back to the door. "Thanks, Susan. I'll be out in a bit and we'll talk."

Susan closed the door behind her and couldn't help noticing the grin she felt plastered across her face.

Adam was back.

~

Adam settled his mom into their suite. She was tired from the trip and wanted to lie down for a bit. He explained how she just needed to walk out the door and down the hallway to the lobby and she'd find him there, or Dorothy would know where he was. He still felt a bit anxious at leaving her alone in a new place.

"Adam, go on. Quit fussing over me. I know you worry about me, but please, let me still have some independence." His mother shooed him out the door and he went in search of Susan.

He found her in the office talking to her computer. "Give me the number. I mean it. You can't hide it from me forever."

He laughed as he entered the room, glad to be back on Belle Island, glad to be back here with Susan. "Does it help when you threaten the computer?"

Susan looked up at him sheepishly. "Sometimes my threats work and the computer obeys, but sometimes it just makes me feel better."

He pulled up a seat and sat backwards, resting his elbows on the chair back. "So can we talk for a bit?"

"Of course." Susan pushed away the offending keyboard.

"I wanted to explain something. I ah... well, why I brought my mother along."

"I'm glad you did."

"She...well..." Adam sighed. It was still hard to say it and the mere word struck fear in his gut. "She was recently diagnosed with Alzheimer's."

"Oh, Adam. I am so sorry." Susan's face crinkled with concern.

"It's early stages, but she did get lost a while ago and now I worry about her all the time. I should have seen the signs, but she's always been kind of scattered and forgetful. After she got lost, I took her to the doctor. They ran a bunch of tests and this is what they came up with." Adam could feel the fear creep up his spine. "I have a caretaker that comes in each day when I'm at work to check on her. She stayed overnight with Mom while I was here before."

"That must be hard for both of you."

"Mom doesn't like people to know. She wants them to just treat her like before. But I wanted you to know just in case you find her... confused at times. I really haven't figured out how to deal with all of this."

He placed his chin on his arms. "But I'm not comfortable leaving her for very long and feel like she needs to be checked on regularly. I got this super easy cell phone that she can push one button and call me if she needs me. I still feel like I need to do more, but without taking away all of her independence."

Susan got up and walked around the desk. She pulled up a chair beside him and rested her hand on his arm. "It must be hard to find the right balance."

"It is." Adam stared at her hand. The fingernails were painted a bright pink, and a simple silver bracelet encircled her wrist. He looked up into her eyes and saw sympathy. "I don't want you to feel sorry for us, Susan. We're doing fine. We take it day by day."

"I don't feel *sorry* for you. I *feel* for you. Different things." Susan squeezed his arm.

He let out a long breath. "And that is why I was trying so hard for the bonus for closing the deal on the inn. Before I figured out that mom was having memory problems, she was swindled out of all of her money. The police are looking into it, but so far no leads. I'll never forgive myself for not checking in on her more and realizing what was happening."

"So she depends on you now?"

"I support her, yes. She'll need a lot of expensive meds and care in the future and I was counting on the bonus to help with that. I've lost that now."

"Oh, Adam. You gave up so much for us."

"It wasn't only for you. It was for me. I couldn't live with myself working with a man with no morals, no ethics." He sighed. "But I've got a mess to figure out now. After we find a way to stop Mr. Burns, I've got to find a new job right away. I'll start looking while we figure out how to stop Mr. Burns from causing any more trouble."

Susan leaned forward and before he knew what was happening, she kissed him gently on the mouth. He reached up and cradled her face with his hand, pulling her closer.

She pulled away after a moment and smiled shyly. "I've been wanting another kiss."

"Me, too." His voice was deep and gravelly. "How about another one?"

CHAPTER 20

The next day Susan, Adam, and Jamie sat at the worn wooden table in the small library at the inn while Adam's mother and Dorothy went to the knitting group. Adam caught Susan staring at him and grinned at her. She looked away quickly, a pretty blush covering her face.

"So we have no idea what Russell is going to try and pull next? He gave you no clue?" Jamie looked at Adam.

"No. There was nothing in the files about what other tricks he had up his sleeve. Mr. Burns kept a lot of things a secret it seems."

"I don't think you need to keep calling him Mr. Burns. He's not your boss anymore." Jamie tossed a wry smile.

"I guess I don't. Russell. I can call him that. I think." Adam grinned, then he felt the grin slip away. "I did find out something before I left though."

"What's that?" Susan frowned.

"Russell is planning… well, he's planning to tear down the inn completely if he buys it."

"No." Both Susan and Jamie said the word in unison.

"He can't. The inn has been part of this island for so long. It's part of its history, just like the lighthouse. We can't let him tear down the inn." Susan's eyes filled with worry.

"All along, I thought he was planning on incorporating it into the resort. Maybe rehab and update a bit, but keep the soul of the inn. *Not so much*. He plans to tear it down and build some kind of modern resort to the limits of size that the island building codes will allow. That's why he also bought the adjoining property."

"We have to stop him." Susan pushed away from the table.

"We will, Mom. He's not going to do this to you, to us." Jamie looked as worried as Susan.

Adam grabbed the pad of paper in front of him. "Okay, first let's make a list of everything we need to get done to fix all the trouble he's already caused.

Then I'm going to make a few calls and see if I can figure out what he's planning next. I should have pumped Mr. Burns—*I mean Russell*—for information before I quit. I was just feeling so self-righteous that I didn't think to find out his plans first."

Jamie took the list when they finished and went to make some phone calls for repairs.

Susan sat lost in thought after Jamie left. Adam secretly watched her as he aimlessly jotted down more items on the writing pad. She looked up and smiled at him, a smile that warmed him and made him feel like he was someone special to her.

Was he special to her?

I could ask her…

Before he could get up his nerve, Susan stood and stretched. "I really should go help Jamie."

He stood beside her and without second guessing himself, he wrapped an arm around her. He pulled her close and she leaned against him. It felt so right to have her here in his arms. He wanted more than anything to take that look of worry away from her eyes. But, to tell the truth, he wasn't sure they were going to be able to stop Russell. The man always seemed to get his way when he set his mind on something, and he sure had his mind set on getting the inn.

〜

Susan could still feel the heat of Adam's body as she walked away from him. She could have stood for hours, just letting him hold her. But that wasn't going to get any of their problems solved. She crossed over to the reception area and told the girl working the desk that she'd take over.

Dorothy and Mary came into the lobby chattering about their knitting group.

"I had the best time. Thank you so much for letting me tag along." Mary set her knitting bag down beside the reception desk.

"It was great to have you there. You're quite the knitter. That lace shawl you're working on is gorgeous." Dorothy set her knitting behind the desk. "We could sit and knit later when my shift is over if you'd like."

"I'd like that very much." Mary smiled.

"I'm glad you two had a good time." Susan clicked a key on the keyboard but nothing happened. She checked the connection. Click. Nothing. "I swear this machine hates me."

Dorothy reached over and clicked the escape key and the computer blinked to life.

"Figures. I think I just don't have the magic touch with the cranky old computer." Susan sighed.

"Don't talk bad to her, or she'll start acting up."
Dorothy grinned.

"I can barely work a cell phone, much less a
computer." Mary laughed. "Well, I think I'll head
back to my room. Might knit some more on the
patio. It's such a gorgeous day. If you see Adam, tell
him where I am."

"He's in the library, I'll tell him when he comes
out." Susan still eyed the computer with a look of
distrust and poked a key on the keyboard to make
sure it was working.

Mary headed down the hallway. Dorothy stared
at Susan and wrinkled her brow. "Hm, you look
all… I don't know. If I didn't know that you were
going through all this trouble with Russell, I'd
almost say you look *happy*."

Susan grinned. "I might be. Well, not about the
inn's problems, of course."

"It's Adam, isn't it? You've forgiven him and you
like him, don't you?"

"I do like him."

"Ha, I knew it!" Dorothy flourished a pen in
triumph. "Oh, and don't forget you're meeting Tally
and Julie tonight. You said to remind you so you
wouldn't be late."

"Yes. Thanks." Susan turned, walked out around
the reception desk, and momentarily froze.

Where the heck was she headed?
Oh, to find Jamie. That's right.

More thinking about what was going on, and less thinking about Adam, that's what she needed to do.

As if that were going to happen…

⁓

Julie carefully set the small table for dinner with her friends. They usually ate at The Sweet Shoppe or Magic Cafe, but Julie liked to cook for them every so often. You'd think she'd get enough cooking and baking at The Sweet Shoppe, but sometimes it was fun to experiment with new recipes for three, instead of big recipes for lots of people at the bakery. She did do a lot of cooking for Reed, too. Cooking was one of the great joys in her life.

"We're here." Tally's voice rang through the small cottage. She and Susan entered the kitchen.

"Smells heavenly." Tally walked over to the stove and peeked in the pot.

"New recipe. I hope it turns out." Julie turned the heat down on the stove and checked the oven. "We have about thirty minutes. We can sit out on the patio, or go up to the widow's walk."

"I'll always choose the widow's walk in nice

weather like this." Susan quickly made the decision for all of them.

They poured glasses of wine, climbed the stairs, and settled into the chairs. Julie glanced at her watch and vowed to keep an eye on the time so everything turned out perfectly. She'd run back downstairs in twenty minutes to check, but for now she settled back in her chair. "I have some news."

"What's that?" Susan took a sip of her wine.

"Well, I know you thought it would never happen, but Reed and I set a wedding date."

"You did? That's wonderful." Tally nodded her head. "Been hoping you'd come to your senses and pick a date. When is it?"

"About six months. The first weekend in April. Susan, I'm hoping to have the wedding at the inn? I did call Jamie to see if you were booked for a wedding that weekend, but I made him promise not to tell you until I had a chance to talk to you." Julie looked at her friend.

"Of course you can. We'd love for you to have it there. We can make that happen. Oh, Julie, I'm so happy for you." Susan raised her wine glass in a toast. "To our Julie actually setting a date for her wedding."

Her friends raised their glasses and Julie was overwhelmed with the warmth of friendship she shared with these two women. She raised her glass and smiled.

These two women had been a lifeline and support system, they pushed her when she needed it, and listened when that was all she wanted. She was one lucky woman to claim Tally and Susan as friends.

After dinner, Tally sat with her two friends, drinking coffee and chatting. "So, we've talked about the wedding, but how about you fill us in on the Adam situation?" Tally peered over her glasses and looked at Susan.

"So we're calling him a situation now?" Susan grinned.

"Call him what you want, but he's back in town and we want the scoop." Julie set down her mug.

"He's here and staying at the inn. He brought his mother with him."

"His mom?" Julie raised an eyebrow.

"He... well, he thought she could use a vacation." Susan looked away, then continued. "She's very nice. She and Dorothy hit it off and they're stealing every minute they can to sit and knit. Oh, or do crossword puzzles. They both love doing the crosswords, too."

Tally didn't miss the strange expression on Susan's face when Julie asked about why Adam brought his mother along, but she brought the subject back to the main course—Adam. "And Adam?"

"Adam is… well, he's trying to help. I'm really worried that Russell is going to succeed. He's trying every underhanded trick in the book to strong-arm us into selling." Susan's eyes flashed in anger. "And you know what Adam found out? Russell is planning on tearing down the inn if he buys it."

"He can't do that." Tally's words were edged in anger and disbelief. "The inn is part of this island."

"I know it is. But Russell doesn't care about that. He wants to build some modern, gleaming, flashy resort."

"Not sure Belle Island is the right location for something like that." Julie shook her head.

"Well, we're not selling if I have anything at all to say about it." Susan set her mug down just a little too forcefully and splashed a bit of coffee on the table.

Julie jumped up and grabbed a towel. "Do you think he'll take no for an answer now? And know you mean it?"

"I think he's simply taking his time thinking up another way to make my life miserable." Susan cleaned up the spilled coffee. "Adam says he's sure Russell hasn't given up."

"So, you and Adam. Anything going on there?" Julie took the towel and hung it up by the sink.

"Well... maybe. I mean, I do like him."

"You more than like him. I can tell." Tally shook her head. "There's no denying it."

"Well, he *did* kiss me."

"Aha!" Julie sank onto her chair. "And was it a spectacular kiss?"

"It was... very nice."

"That's all?" Tally eyed her friend.

"Okay, okay, it was wonderful and I admit I'm a *bit* taken with the man. A *lot* taken. But he's only here for a bit and there are other... complications. So I'm just taking it one day at a time."

Tally didn't miss the way her friend's eyes lit up when she talked about Adam. She was almost positive that Susan was more than just taken with Adam. She was pretty sure Susan was falling in love, whether she realized it yet or not.

CHAPTER 21

The next morning, Susan felt like she was being torn in ten different directions. Three people called in sick. Julie's delivery van had broken down, so she'd sent Jamie to get their baked goods for the day and help Julie with the rest of her deliveries. The coffee delivery was two days late, and they were down to just enough for breakfast. *Maybe.* Their coffee beans came from a small local company, but they'd been having supply issues, and as much as Susan hated it, she might have to change to a different company. In the meantime, she'd asked Jamie to pick up coffee, too.

She was supposed to meet with Adam later this morning, but she didn't know how that was going to happen. Adam and Mary walked into the dining

165

room as she was pouring coffee for some of her guests.

Adam's face broke into a big smile when he saw her, a smile that made her heart beat faster and her pulse pound in her ears. She motioned for them to take a seat by the window. As soon as she could, she grabbed some menus and dropped them off at their table. "Sorry. We're short staffed in the kitchen and in here. Things are a bit nuts right now."

"I could help." Mary looked up at Susan.

"Oh, I couldn't ask you to do that."

"I don't see why not. I'm perfectly able to deliver food, clear tables, refresh people's coffee, or whatever you need me to do."

"Mom, I don't think that's such—"

"Adam, don't treat me like I'll break. I can help. I *want* to help." Mary's voice was firm and confident.

"I don't know…" Adam's face was covered in doubt.

Susan stepped in where she probably wasn't wanted, because it wasn't her decision to make. "I'd love some help."

Adam looked at her pointedly. She just as pointedly looked back at him.

Mary jumped up. "Great. Get me started on anything that will help you out."

"Well, that table over there that just came in needs water. The glasses and pitchers of water are on the sideboard along with the coffee if they want that."

"Perfect. And I see that table over there needs to be cleared. I'll get that, too." Mary hurried off to the sideboard.

"I'm not sure this is a good idea." Adam looked at Susan.

"I think you should let her try if she wants. Everyone wants to feel useful. You said she was in very early stages of her disease. Let her help. I'll keep an eye on her."

Adam still didn't look totally convinced. He glanced over in his mother's direction and sighed. "Okay. You both win. I know she does like to keep busy."

"Great." Susan started to walk away but felt Adam's hand on her arm.

"Before you go. I was wondering where you keep the old records for the inn. I'd like to look at them. I might have an idea, but I don't want to get your hopes up. Do you mind if I look at the records?"

"No, not at all if you think it might help. We keep them in file cabinets and boxes up in the attic area. There's a small room up there with a window, but it's kind of stuffy. There's an old desk and lamp you can use. I'm not sure what all is stored up there."

"Perfect. I'll head up and poke around a bit."

"Any idea anyone comes up with to thwart Russell is fine with me. I appreciate the help."

"I'm your man."

Susan smiled to herself. He wasn't exactly her man, but she certainly liked having him around.

"Mom, I got the coffee." Jamie set a large sack of coffee beans on the counter in the kitchen.

"Thanks." One problem averted for now.

"We got Julie's van towed and I told her she could use the inn's van for a few days while they fix hers. I figured that was okay with you." Jamie helped himself to a pastry on the counter.

"That's great. She'll need one for her deliveries. That van of hers is on its last leg, or last miles, or whatever a really-too-old-to-be-driving vehicle is. Of course, ours isn't much better."

Jamie poured himself a cup of coffee and lounged against the counter. "I talked to Harry, and he gave me the name of a contractor to contact to convert another room to handicapped on the first floor. Harry had a good idea. If we use that one guest room that's beside the small storage area, we can convert the storage area into a bigger bathroom for the handicapped room. I'll get quotes on it in the next few days. We'll get the bigger doorway to the room that way, too. Harry says this contractor is really reasonable."

"Thanks for checking into all of that. At least that will solve one of our problems."

Jamie took a gulp of coffee. "I saw Mary out there clearing a table."

"She offered to help and I said yes. We're short staffed today, and you were gone helping Julie. Adam is off looking at old files in the attic."

"Really? What for?" Jamie took another big swig of coffee and downed the rest of the pastry in two bites.

Susan rolled her eyes. The boy—okay, *man* now —could devour food like a hungry wolf. "I'm not sure exactly what he's looking for. He just said that he had an idea on a way to stop Russell."

Jamie shrugged. "Okay then. I'll go set up the beach umbrellas and be back in to help in a jiffy." Jamie pushed away from the counter and sauntered out of the kitchen.

Susan couldn't help the swell of pride she felt at seeing the wonderful man he'd become. In spite of the mistakes she made as a mother, in spite of losing his father at such a young age, and in spite of the difficulties Jamie had had with Russell as a stepfather, he'd turned out fine. Better than fine. She couldn't imagine a better future than sharing the responsibilities of running the inn with her son.

She turned back to washing the dishes, one other job on her to-do list today since the kitchen helper had called in sick. Her mind lost in a tangle of thoughts about Adam, Russell, and the inn's problems, she methodically went through the motions of rinsing the dishes.

"Susan, we have a problem." Dorothy stood by her side with a worried look on her face.

That look caused a momentary panic to race through Susan. Dorothy rarely let anything ruffle her feathers.

"I was opening the mail and sorting through it like I always do. You got this letter." Dorothy held out a piece of paper.

Susan took it and saw the bank's letterhead. She frowned. They weren't behind on any payments. She unfolded the paper and stared at the words.

Your improvement loan was sold to an investor. According to the terms, an appraiser will be out to assess the property to ensure the value of the inn is greater than your outstanding loans.

Susan looked at Dorothy. "I'm not sure why they sold our secondary loan, but I don't think this will be a problem. I know the value of the inn is greater than the loans. It always has been, and it's not like all of a sudden it's gone down in value." Susan frowned. "I wonder why they sold the loan papers. I guess they're wanting more capital. I'll give Jim at the bank a call in the next few days and see what's up."

"So you think it's just a coincidence that this is happening now?"

"Oh, I don't see how Russell could have anything to do with this. Why would he buy up the secondary loan if he wants to buy the whole inn? Makes no sense." Susan shook her head. "Anyway, let me know if the appraiser shows up."

"Will do." Dorothy left, and Susan folded the paper and stuck it in her pocket. She made a mental note to call the bank.

Susan sat on the deck at the end of a long day.

Hopefully, all the employees would be back tomorrow. She got so far behind on her own work when she had to fill in for missing workers.

She sat with her feet propped up on the railing, sipping a beer. The moonlight slashed a pathway of silvery light across the waves and spilled onto the beach. All was quiet now with just an occasional couple strolling by in the moonlight.

"May I join you?" Adam stood next to her chair, a beer in hand.

"Of course." Susan's pulse quickened as she motioned to the empty chair beside her.

Adam sat and stretched his long legs up on the railing beside hers. She noticed he'd switched attire from business slacks and button-down shirts from his working for Russell days, to casual shorts and sandals.

She watched while he took a swig of his beer from a longneck bottle. The moonlight illuminated him. A hint of a shadow of a day's growth of whiskers covered the chiseled contours of his face.

"Long day for you, wasn't it?" Adam's deep voice rolled over her, and she pulled it around her like a security blanket.

"It was, but we got through it. Your mom was a big help. She just never quit. By tonight she was taking orders at the restaurant. She must be exhausted."

"She is, but she was so happy when I talked to her this evening. You know, I think I'm overprotecting her a bit too much. I do worry about her ever since she got lost, but she seems to be doing okay. To be honest, she was in a new area of Atlanta and anyone could get lost there. I think she was as much overwhelmed with all the changes in her life as anything else. I do want her to have as normal a life as she can, for as long as she can."

"Alzheimer's is such an ugly disease." Susan stared at the ocean, wondering what it would be like to know that you were going to lose your ability to remember things. To remember places. To remember the names and faces of the people you loved. To watch all that slip away. To know what your loved ones were going to go through watching you slip way.

"It is ugly and unfair. Mom is the best, kindest person. Life just throws you curves sometimes, and you have to deal with them as best as you can. I waver from being angry for her lot in life and feeling very sad. I plan on being there for her every single step of the way, though."

"You're a good son."

"Well except for letting her get swindled out of

all her money. No, if I'd been a good son and paying attention, I wouldn't have let some shyster dupe her out of her life's savings."

Adam sat back and rubbed his face. "I was so busy working, and I didn't visit enough or keep up with what was going on in her life. By the time I did, she'd lost everything."

"That's terrible when people take advantage of older people like that."

"It is. I just don't understand people sometimes."

"Me neither." Susan immediately thought of Russell. Speaking of not understanding people, why was he so intent of buying the inn? There had to be lots of properties better suited. Was it just his twisted revenge? But he was the one who had wanted the divorce. He'd basically gotten everything. So why couldn't he just leave her well enough alone now?

"You okay?" Adam eyed her with concern. "You look... I'm not sure... upset?"

"I was thinking about Russell. He left me. He divorced me. He got everything. I don't know why he now wants to take away the one thing that is mine."

"He's pretty ruthless." Adam stated the obvious.

"I know you're wondering why I ever married

him. He wasn't always like that. At least he wasn't with me. After Jamie's father died I really struggled. Emotionally and financially. I know it doesn't make logical sense, but I was *so angry* that he left me. Not that it was his choice. He died in an accident at work. He did construction. They were working on a building and it collapsed and killed four workers."

"I'm sorry. That must have been hard."

"It was. I was young, Jamie was young. I had no family except for my brother. I worked long hours. I finally found the job at Russell's company and started making better money. I guess I caught his eye, because he started asking me out. I kept saying no because... well, he was the owner. Finally I agreed to go out with him. He treated me well and showered me with presents. I liked him. I mean, I never loved him like I did Jamie's father, but I cared for Russell." Susan took a sip of her beer and couldn't help the sigh that escaped.

"Russell asked me to marry him and I said yes. I knew I'd be able to give Jamie a better life. After the first few years, though, it got... rocky. He never did like Jamie much, which if I had known that before we got married, I never would have married him. He'd always been nice enough to Jamie when we dated, but he didn't like having a child in the house. Jamie could never do anything right. I did my best to protect him from Russell's thoughtless remarks, which got crueler as Jamie got older."

Susan felt the tears at the corners of her eyes. "I should have left Russell years ago. Gotten Jamie out of that house. As it was, I sent him down here to Belle Island every summer. He loved it here. Then he went away to college and never came home except for an occasional holiday, and then he'd only stay a day or two."

Adam reached over and took her hand in his. "We all regret some of the choices we make, the roads we take. But we all have to learn to live with our decisions."

Adam couldn't help but notice the tears glistening in Susan's eyes. The full moon illuminated them like a silvery daylight.

He leaned over and trailed his hand up her arm and back down while she stared out to sea, lost in her thoughts. Her skin warmed beneath his touch. He looked around the deck and saw they were all alone.

He held open his arms to her. "Come here."

She looked at him, slowly got up as if warring with herself, then settled down on his lap. He pulled her close, stroking her arm, feeling her hair brush across his face like a silk scarf. He kissed her lips gently and she sighed, snuggling in closer.

If he could freeze this moment, freeze this feeling, then everything would be perfect.

But reality wouldn't let that happen. There was the responsibility of taking care of his mother. One he didn't mind, but always hung over him with the fear he couldn't truly help her. There was Russell to thwart.

Then there was one more huge, scary problem. He'd heard the love and fondness in her voice when she'd talked about Jamie's father. He wondered if she'd ever love another man like she'd loved her first husband.

And that thought made him incredibly sad, because as much as he didn't want to admit it, he was falling in love with this woman.

CHAPTER 22

Susan sat at the dressing table in her room, brushing her hair. She swore she could still feel the heat of the kiss Adam had given her last night when he'd walked her to her door. The kiss had stirred up long forgotten feelings. Feelings she never thought she'd know again.

But, she needed to be careful. There was no way she was going through falling for a man who was just going to leave her. She'd done that. Twice. She didn't intend to make it three times, and Adam would leave soon to take a job where he could support his mother and take care of her.

She reached up to touch her cheek. A flicker of happiness and a wash of melancholia hit her at the same time, if that was even possible. He made her heart flip when she saw him, and that scared her.

She could talk herself out of liking the man, right?

It had been years and years since Jamie's father had died, years and years since she'd known that overwhelming and complete love. The kind that made you whole. The kind that surged through your entire being. The kind you were completely and utterly sure of.

The kind of love that she was deathly afraid she was beginning to feel for Adam.

Susan hurried down to the kitchen to make sure everything was running smoothly. She caught Julie as she was delivering their baked goods for the day. She gave her friend a quick hug.

"Things going better this morning?" Susan pressed a cup of coffee into Julie's hands.

"Much. Thanks for the loan of your van. Mine should be fixed in a few days. At least I hope it can. I haven't budgeted for a new delivery van, though I should consider putting it in next year's budget. The old gal can't go on forever."

"Well, hopefully you can keep it limping along."

"I'm going to keep my eye open for used vans for sale. Maybe I'll find a good deal." Julie sighed and sipped the hot coffee. "So good. I wonder who invented coffee? Whoever it was, he's a saint in my book."

Susan laughed. "Coffee is one of those gifts from the universe, isn't it?"

"So what's up with you and Adam?" Julie gave her the side eye.

"Nothing. Well, the same. I mean. I don't know what I mean."

Julie grinned. "That's what I thought. You're falling for him."

"No, I'm being careful that I don't fall for him." Susan said each word with emphasis so that maybe she could convince herself along with Julie.

Julie shrugged. "If you say so. Sometimes our hearts don't listen to our heads, though."

"Mine will. I'm not going to go down that road again. I have a good life here. I don't need any entanglements, especially with someone who is leaving soon."

"Well, I'm not one to give you advice on that, since I fell for Reed within weeks, and he was supposed to leave Belle Island. Love does funny things to our well-planned lives."

"Who said anything about love?" Susan glared at her friend.

Julie grinned back at her. "No one. But I've known you a long time. You can't hide it from me, even if you can try to hide it from yourself. You've fallen for him."

Susan scowled. "I have not." She sighed. "Well, maybe a little."

"Told you." Julie shoved off the counter and put down her coffee cup. "I've got more deliveries. I'll see you soon."

"Okay, see you soon."

Susan watched her friend walk out to the van and drive away. She hadn't been able to convince Julie that she wasn't letting her heart get involved with Adam, but she sure as heck was going to convince herself of that very thing.

She turned at the sound of Jamie's voice. "Mom, the appraiser guy is here. I have a copy of his work order... and I thought you'd want to see it." He thrust the paper into her hand, a look of protective fierceness firmly in place on his scowling face.

She looked at the page. It was a simple request for an appraisal. As she scanned down the paper she froze.

Adam. It was signed by Adam. She looked up

and searched Jamie's face. "I don't get it. Why would Adam's signature be on the appraisal form?"

She bit her lip. "Unless... you don't think he's really still working for Russell, do you?"

"I did an internet search on this third party investment company. It's one of Russell's holdings. Not sure what other explanation there is." Jamie's eyes flashed with anger. "I don't think he's really here to help us. I think he's here to throw us off track while they finish destroying us."

Susan's heart fell to the depths of her soul. She'd been so wrapped up in Adam's interest in her, she'd convinced herself he liked her. It was probably all part of his plan. He'd tricked her again. When was she ever going to learn? A shutter dropped on her emotions and she closed them off. She was done with this nonsense. Done with men. Finished.

Adam rushed into the kitchen and pulled up short at the look on Susan's face when she turned to him. Where he was used to seeing a welcoming smile and even a hint of a blush, he saw flashing eyes and a murderous expression.

He'd have to sort that out in a minute, for now he needed her help.

"Adam, we need to talk."

"Okay, we will. I can see you're upset. But it will have to be later."

"No, it needs to be now." Jamie walked up to his mother's side and placed an arm around her shoulder.

Adam ignored the obvious fact that both of them were angry and blurted out his words. "Listen, I need your help. Have either of you seen my mother?"

The hard edges of Susan's expression softened into a look of concern. "Not this morning."

"I can't find her anywhere. I've looked in the room, on the deck, in the restaurant." He scrubbed his hand over his face and swallowed. "She's not answering her cell phone, though that's not unusual. The cell phone seems to confuse her a bit."

"She's probably around somewhere. Let me call Dorothy's cell phone and see if she's with her." Susan pulled out her phone and dialed. "Dorothy, we're looking for Mary. Have you seen her?"

Susan's frown gave him his answer.

"Okay, if you see her give me a call." Susan slipped the phone back in her pocket. "Did you check the library?"

"I did."

"Maybe she went for a walk." Jamie didn't look

too worried about a grown woman being gone for a bit.

Susan looked at Adam, searching his face, and he nodded. Susan turned to Jamie. "Son, Mary has Alzheimer's. She's already gotten lost once. We need to find her and make sure she's okay."

A look of surprise spread over Jamie's face. "I'm sorry. I had no idea. Of course, I'll help look for her."

"I don't know what to do." Adam stood paralyzed with fear. Would she try to swim and get confused? Did she go for a walk and get lost?

Susan placed her hand on his arm. "We'll find her. Come on, let's all split up."

"Jamie, you search the inn again then maybe look around town. Adam, you head down the beach, I'll head towards Lighthouse Point. Call if anyone finds her."

Adam was grateful for someone taking charge. His mind was in panic mode. He hurried outside with Susan, and they took off in opposite directions. He quickened his pace into a jog as he hurried down the beach.

Susan walked at a brisk pace, looking up toward the

homes and along the shoreline. The wind whipped her hair in her face, and she wished she'd brought a hairband to keep it out of the way. She rounded the bend to Lighthouse Point and saw Mary standing near the lighthouse. She hurried up the beach to reach her.

"Mary, there you are." Susan gasped her words and leaned over to catch her breath.

"Why, hello, dear. Are you taking a walk, too? It's a glorious day for it."

"I, uh. Well, I was looking for you. Adam was worried when he couldn't find you."

Mary frowned. "I do wish he'd just… let me live a little. I know he's worried about me. He means well, but he's smothering me."

"I think he's just concerned…"

Mary looked directly at Susan and cocked her head to the side. "So, he told you, didn't he? I asked him not to say anything. I don't want people treating me differently."

"I think he just wants to make sure you're safe. He told me so I would look out for you, too. He loves you. He's trying to be a good son."

Mary sighed. "I know that. I did worry him that one day when I was so confused and got lost. But, really, it was an area I wasn't familiar with and they'd done all this construction, and I couldn't get my bearings."

Susan took Mary's hand in hers. "He's worried about you."

"I know. He's a good son. I don't know how to explain to him that I need to live my life as fully as I can... for as long as I can. And I don't know how much longer that will be." Mary's eyes clouded over. "It's scary, the not knowing what's coming next and how it will be for me, but it has given me a strong appreciation for every single minute of the day. Today was so beautiful, I just wanted to wander down the beach a bit. I wanted to feel the freedom."

"Let me text Adam and tell him you're okay. We'll walk back together, okay?"

"Okay, dear. I didn't mean to worry anyone."

"I know you didn't. Maybe just leave a note for Adam next time so he doesn't worry."

Mary sighed. "I should have. I just didn't think of it. I will next time." Mary paused and looked directly at Susan. "You don't think I'm a silly old woman for wanting this time to myself... the chance to do what I want, when I want? The chance to have a little bit of freedom?"

Susan hugged the older woman. "Not silly at all. I don't pretend to know what you're going through, but I think you have the right to deal with it in whatever way works for you."

Mary smiled a little smile. "I don't suppose you could talk to Adam and convince him to give me a bit of space…"

"I'll do that, I promise."

Right before I kick his sorry carcass to the curb for coming back here and spying on us.

CHAPTER 23

Adam met Susan and his mother at the stairs to the deck and wrapped his mother in a big bear hug.

"Mom, I was so worried."

"Adam, I *am* allowed to go for a walk. I don't want you watching me like a hawk all the day long."

"But, Mom, you need—"

"I think you should listen to your mother, Adam." Susan looked at him pointedly. "She's trying to make you understand."

He turned to his mother and held his words.

"Son, I know you mean well, but you have to give me some freedom. But I will leave you a note if I leave the inn again. Is that a fair compromise?"

Adam took his mother's hands in his. "Yes, it is.

189

And I will try and give you your space. I will." But it would be hard. Very hard. He wanted to wrap her up and protect her from what the future held in store for her.

"Well, I'm tired now and I think I'll go take a little rest." Mary turned to Susan. "But I'll be up and ready to help you this afternoon."

Adam took his mother's arm and started up the stairs to the deck.

"Adam, when you get your mother settled, can I see you, please?" He turned back to see the angry look plastered across Susan's face again. He didn't miss the icy tone in her voice either.

He nodded. "I'll come see you as soon as I get Mom all settled in. I'll meet you at your office."

Susan nodded curtly, twirled, and walked around the side of the inn, disappearing between the palm trees.

He sighed. He was bone weary from worry over his mother, and now something was obviously wrong with Susan.

If life would like to show him just a little break today, that would be great.

"So was it all a game to you? Was it Russell's idea

for you to bring your mother so we'd accept you more readily?" Susan clutched the edge of her desk and faced down Adam.

"What do you mean? I quit that job. You know that." Adam wearily rubbed his face.

"Really?" Susan snatched a paper off the desk.

"You didn't sign this request for an appraiser to come evaluate the inn for the company that bought our secondary loan?"

"No, I don't know what you're talking about." Adam eyed her warily.

She held out the crinkled paper. "Isn't that your signature? Didn't you authorize the appraiser?"

Adam looked at the page. "Well, that's my signature, but it was for a private inspector to come out and quickly appraise the inn for us if you signed the deal with Russell. I didn't know anything about this secondary loan."

Susan wasn't sure she believed him. She *didn't* believe him. His name was right there in black and white. "Our secondary loan was bought out by a third party. They want an appraisal to make sure the value of the inn is greater than our loans."

"Who bought it out?" Adam scanned the paper. She could tell the moment he grasped what was going on. He looked up at her. "You mean Russell bought out the secondary loan?"

"Looks that way, doesn't it?"

She watched his face carefully the whole time, wanting more than anything to believe he had nothing to do with this, but unwilling to be made a fool. *Again*.

"What can I do to convince you I didn't know about this?"

"The sad thing is, I'm not sure there is anything you can do to truly make me believe you now." Susan walked to the door of the office. "I have work to do."

Adam walked up to her and brushed past, only a fraction of an inch away from her. Electricity crackled between them, but she convinced herself it was only from her anger and their confrontation.

He handed her the paper and their hands touched ever so briefly. He looked directly into her eyes. "You should believe in me. I'm telling you the truth."

She watched him walk across the lobby with slow and measured steps. She wanted to believe him, she did. But how could she? She needed to be very careful or she was going to lose the inn. She had no room for missteps.

~

Tally sat in Susan's office sipping a drink. The cubes clinked around in the glass of sweet tea. "I only have a few minutes, but since I was going right past the inn, I thought I'd drop in and see how you're doing."

"You always seem to have an instinct for when we need you, don't you? I've been better. It appears Russell bought our secondary mortgage, or the investment company he owns part of did."

Tally sat up straight. "No."

"Yes. So an appraiser is coming to look at the inn and guess whose name is on the appraisal request authorizing it?"

"Russell's?" Tally frowned.

"No, Adam's."

Tally set down her tea. "I thought he quit his job with Russell and came back to help."

"Well, that's what he said, but now I'm not sure."

"Did you ask him about it?" Tally was all for taking the direct approach with people.

"He said the request he put in was for an appraisal if we sold to Russell. He said he didn't know about the buyout of the loan."

"And did you believe him?"

"He looked sincere, but honestly, I can't make any mistakes. We're too close to losing everything

193

we worked for. I'm thinking of asking him to leave, but I do hate to kick out Mary. She and Dorothy have really hit it off." Susan jabbed a wayward curl back from her face.

Tally looked at her friend and decided now was one of those times to speak her mind. "Do you think that maybe, just maybe, you're thinking of asking him to leave because you're afraid?"

"Yes, I'm afraid I'll lose the inn."

"No, I think you're afraid you'll lose your *heart*." Tally leaned forward. "I think you're falling in love with the man and that scares you just as much as losing the inn scares you… if not more."

Susan sat and tapped a pencil on her desk. "No, that's not it." She frowned. "At least I don't think it is… *is it?*"

"I think that you're afraid of getting hurt. Afraid he's one more man who is going to leave you. I think that you're afraid to take a chance." Tally stood. "I think you should listen to your heart. Adam is a good guy. I'm a pretty good judge of character, and I believe you can trust him. Life is messy sometimes and we have to take that leap of faith. Take a risk."

"I don't know if I can…" Susan's voice was almost a whisper.

"Only you can make that decision." Tally spun

around and walked out the door, leaving her friend alone with her thoughts and decisions.

Tally only hoped that Susan would listen to her. Tally knew what it was like to not take a risk, and to lose it all.

CHAPTER 24

The next couple of days were awkward. Adam tried his best to allay Susan's fears and get her to believe in him. She'd even mentioned that it would be okay for him to leave and go back to Atlanta to search for work. She didn't quite say he *had* to leave, so he didn't. He wasn't ready to give up on her, or the inn.

He wasn't ready to take his mother back to Atlanta, either. She was thriving in this environment. She helped around the inn and spent the afternoons or evenings knitting with Dorothy, depending on Dorothy's schedule.

He did the odd job around the inn to help out, but he wasn't much of a fix-it man. He was a negotiator, a manager, and he knew a lot about running big resorts but nothing about running a small inn. He continued to sort through files up in the attic, not quite sure what he was looking for.

His mother had gone to bed early tonight, so he grabbed a beer from the bar and went outside to sit on the beach. The stars were tossed like a million diamonds scattered across the sky. They never had views like this in Atlanta with all the city lights obscuring the night sky.

He leaned back on his elbows and watched the waves slowly rolling up on the shore, one after the other, an endless pattern of perseverance. He should take a lesson from the sea and keep trying with Susan. He wasn't ready to give up, but she wasn't making it easy.

He looked up and saw a lone woman walking in the moonlight. He'd know her walk anywhere, the way she swung her arms when she walked, the meandering pattern and stops to pick up shells, the way the breeze tossed the curls around her face. He sat silently and watched as Susan approached, her shadow following along beside her in the strong moonlight.

Then she saw him and within seconds recognized him. He could tell the exact moment.

She froze, looked back over her shoulder as if looking for an escape route, then slowly continued towards him.

Her reluctant steps took her right to where he was sitting, as if the universe had decided to give him one more chance.

And he was going to grab that chance with both hands and hold tight.

"Will you join me?"

"I should get inside."

"Just for a few minutes?"

He watched as she hesitated, then nodded slightly and dropped to the sand beside him but keeping her distance.

"The sky here is amazing. All the stars. The moonlight. I'm not sure I've ever seen anything quite like this." He figured talking about the view was a safe subject.

"It is beautiful." Her words were low and hushed.

He took a deep breath. "Susan, I wish you'd believe me. I had nothing to do with that secondary loan being bought out by Russell's investment group."

Susan turned to look at him, the moonlit skies clearly illuminating her face. "I… I do believe you.

At least I want to. I've been thinking some the last few days." She picked up a handful of sand and let it slip through her fingers. "And Tally gave me a good talking to. She does that."

He kept silent and let her talk.

"She thinks that maybe I'm pushing you away, not because I think you're still working for Russell, but because I'm afraid to…" She looked right into his eyes, into his soul. "I'm afraid to let myself care about you."

She reached a hand across and touched his face. He was certain the touch would brand him for life. He reached up and covered her hand with his.

"I am afraid to care about you. I'm afraid of my feelings for you. I'm afraid… because you'll have to leave soon." She continued to look right into his eyes. "But, the thing is, I *do* care about you, no matter how I try and convince myself that I don't."

He reached over, pulled her close, and kissed her gently on her ever-so-soft lips. A growl escaped him. "Ah, I care about you, too. I care *a lot* about you. It's messy and confusing, we started off wrong, and, yes, I need to go find a job. But none of that matters to me." He pulled her close to his side and wrapped his arms around her. She leaned into him and they sat silently watching the stars and the waves.

He was certain it was the most perfect moment in his entire life.

And though he wasn't ready to tell her yet, he was also certain he was falling in love with her.

CHAPTER 25

The next morning Susan stood in her office, sorting the mail. A letter from the bank caught her eye. Now what?

She slowly slit the envelope with the letter opener and pulled out the page.

As you were informed previously, your improvement loan was sold to an investor. They are exercising their option to call the loan for payment in full, according to the terms you agreed to when you signed the callable loan. You have thirty days to pay off the outstanding balance.

Susan stared at the page. They'd been able to make the payments every month, plus some months even put some extra money towards the loan. But they sure didn't have the cash to pay it off in full.

When she'd taken the loan, she knew it was a callable loan, but the bank had insisted they rarely called a loan unless someone got behind on payments. It had been a gamble they'd taken when loans were hard to come by. Now they were paying the price.

She sank into her chair, the paper mocking her while she clutched it tightly in her hand. While they could overcome Russell's other shenanigans, this one would put them under.

For the first time, Susan considered that maybe they should take Russell's offer, if he was still even willing to buy the inn. At least that way Jamie would be protected. He'd have some money to get started on a new business. If they waited until the bank foreclosed, they'd get nothing.

A surge of despair washed over her and pounded her like storm waves on the sand, breaking everything in its path.

If only she'd never met Russell. This was all her fault, because she'd brought him into their lives.

She released the paper and it floated down to the desk.

Russell had won, and she had lost everything.

Susan wandered aimlessly along the coastline. She hadn't been able to bring herself to tell Jamie yet. He was going to be devastated. He'd worked so hard on making the inn a success, and it was, in its own way. They were slowly making progress with it. Jamie's projections had them actually making a good profit on it in the near future. But Russell was going to take all of that away from them.

Guilt washed over her. For bringing Russell into their lives. For not protecting her son from Russell. Jamie was going to feel like a failure, and Russell would bring that point home, she had no doubt.

She rounded the bend in the shore and saw the lighthouse standing proud and tall, calling her. She continued down the beach until she stood in the shadow of the lighthouse. "I don't believe in your legend, you know." She stood with her hands on her hips, glaring at the lighthouse.

The lighthouse didn't answer her, of course. She wasn't sure what she was supposed to get out of an argument with a lighthouse. She sighed and walked to the water's edge. A bright, perfect shell twinkled in the sunlight. She reached down, scooped it up, and turned it over. A pattern that looked like an S traced through the back of the shell, like it was made just for her.

She glanced at the lighthouse and sighed. "You win."

She closed her eyes and made a wish. "I wish that we could find a way to save the inn."

She opened her eyes and threw the shell into the ocean, then turned to the lighthouse. "There, are you happy?"

She was probably a bit crazy because she could *almost* hear the lighthouse's reply.

"*Yes, I am.*"

Adam threw open the window to air out the attic room. He'd been lugging boxes down to his room to look at them, but it was time to get serious about sorting through the papers up here. He grabbed an old cloth and dusted off the wooden desk so he'd have a place to work. He moved boxes that were blocking the file cabinets and riffled through the files to get an idea of what kind of paperwork had been kept. Someone, Susan's brother he guessed, had carefully organized the files. He dug through them until he found some papers regarding the original inn property and building.

He grabbed those files and stacked them on the desk.

The start of a plan flickered in the recesses of his mind. He sat at the desk and carefully started reading. If they could find the right documentation, maybe, just maybe, he could save the inn from Russell.

Two hours later he was hot, thirsty, and still wasn't sure he had what he needed. He wanted to take some notes before he stopped and took a break. He jerked open a drawer and dug around for a pen and paper. The drawer hung a bit, but he jiggled it until it slid wide open. An official looking, very aged envelope rested in the drawer. He took it out and flipped it over.

The name Hall was scrawled across it in the handwriting of generations past. He pried open the end and slipped out the papers. The pages were weathered and crinkly with age.

He read through the pages with some difficulty, deciphering the words in the fancy script writing. He shuffled through to the last pages and his eyes grew wide. If these were real and hadn't been replaced or reported missing... Would that even be possible?

He shoved everything back into the envelope and bounded down the stairs to find Susan. Maybe, just maybe, he'd found a way to make up for the mess he had made.

CHAPTER 26

Adam looked around the lobby and saw Jamie talking to a well-dress man and woman. He hurried over to them.

"Excuse me, I don't mean to interrupt…"

"Yet, you are. Can't you see that Delbert is talking to Jamie?" The woman flipped her hair behind her shoulder in dismissal.

"Ah, sorry." Adam took a step back.

"No, that's okay. I won't keep Jamie any longer. I was actually looking for his wife, Cindy. I have files to go over with her." The man smiled at Adam and made him feel less like a clod for interrupting.

Jamie shot Adam an apologetic look.

The man stared at Adam for a moment. "I believe we've met?"

Jamie jumped in. "I should introduce you. Mr. Hamilton, Camille, this is Adam Lyons. Adam, this is Camille Montgomery and Mr. Hamilton."

Mr. Hamilton's eyes flickered with recognition, then he smiled. "Ah, I believe I know Mr. Lyons. He outbid me on negotiating for buying a hotel— The Martmont in Charleston, I believe."

Adam looked at the man. He remembered the company he had worked for at the time, before he'd worked for Russell, had been in steep competition when The Martmont had gone up for sale.

"I consider myself a good negotiator, but you did a fine job with your proposal." Mr. Hamilton held out his hand.

Adam shook it. "Well, thanks. It was a tough deal to win."

"Anyway, it was nice to meet you again. Maybe we'll meet across a negotiating table again." Mr. Hamilton turned to the woman at his side. "Camille, I still do need to talk with Cindy."

Camille let out a long, drawn-out sigh. "Well, I'll go get a glass of wine at the bar and wait for you. Don't be long. Mama is expecting company for dinner tonight and I want to get there early to get ready."

"I won't be long."

"Good." Camille spun on her very high heels,

clicked her way across the wooden floor of the lobby, and disappeared into the lounge.

"Cindy is in the library, it's right through there." Jamie pointed the way.

"Thank you." Delbert smiled and headed to find Cindy.

Adam couldn't wait to tell Susan his news. "Where's your mother? I have to talk to her."

"She went for a walk. Seemed a bit out of sorts." Jamie eyed him suspiciously.

"Wasn't me. I swear. We're actually getting along… um… just fine." It was Susan's decision to tell Jamie whatever she wanted him to know about their relationship.

A man in a well-worn suit entered the lobby. Grand central station here today. Adam just wanted to find Susan and tell her the news.

Jamie turned to the man. "May I help you?"

"I'm looking for Susan Hall."

"May I ask why?" Jamie sounded protective.

"I have… private business with her." The man shifted from one foot to the other.

"If it's about the inn, I can deal with it. We're both owners."

"Ah, no… it's personal."

Adam looked at the man and wondered what in

the world this was about. Susan couldn't really take another curve ball right now.

～

Cindy sat at the table in the library where she'd spread her files on rehabbing The Hamilton. She had estimates and was running the numbers for her final presentation to Mr. Hamilton. She'd brought her work home this afternoon to make sure that she'd be here to have dinner with Jamie. They hadn't had dinner together in days, and she'd promised him tonight they would. It seemed a safe bet if she brought her work home, they'd manage a meal together.

She looked up when someone entered the library. "Mr. Hamilton." She jumped up and looked at the mess spread before her. She'd scooped up all the files from work and had just dumped them on the table. She hadn't had a chance yet to sort them all out. He was going to think she was a disorganized slob. She reached down and shoved a bunch of papers into a stack.

"I just wanted to stop by and check on things. I called the hotel and they said you'd come back here. Camille and I were just headed to her mother's."

"Oh, I thought she'd left."

"She changed her mind. She does that." Mr. Hamilton smiled.

"I brought work home tonight so I can run the final estimates. I'll be ready tomorrow to show you your options."

"That sounds great."

She reached down and swept up more papers, desperate to make it look like she was organized. All she managed to do was make the stack of papers slide off the table and onto the floor.

"Oh." She bent down to retrieve the escapees.

Mr. Hamilton crossed over and knelt beside her, helping to gather up the papers. "Let me help."

The man was going to think she was too disorganized to handle the job. She reached for more papers, actually crawling under the table to retrieve them. Embarrassment flushed through her. As she crawled back out from under the table, she saw that Mr. Hamilton had sat back on his heels, staring at a paper in his hand.

She moved over closer to him to see which estimate had made him pause. She froze when she saw the paper he was reading.

"I... um..." Cindy swallowed. "Camille dropped that when she was at my office. I was going to give it back to her. It must have gotten mixed in with my papers..."

Mr. Hamilton stood up and reached a hand down. Cindy took it and awkwardly got to her feet.

He took another look at the paper, folded it carefully, and put it in the breast pocket of his suit coat.

"I'm sorry…" She felt like an idiot.

"There is no reason to be sorry. Nothing is your fault."

"I feel responsible for… well, it's Camille's…" Cindy didn't know what to say. Why did she have to be in the middle of this? She wanted to sink into the floor and fade away. But that was how the old Cindy dealt with problems.

She took a deep breath. "I'm sorry. It was none of my business. I should have made a point to return it to her, but I thought she'd left town. I also was worried that she'd be upset that I'd seen it. Anyway, it shouldn't have gotten mixed in with my papers."

"Don't worry about it anymore. I'll handle it and make sure Camille gets it." Mr. Hamilton had a calm look plastered on his face, and Cindy couldn't tell if he really was not shocked by a past due notice of that amount, or whether he was just practiced at hiding his emotions.

Anyway she looked at it though, she was glad it was no longer her problem.

"I'll see you tomorrow about ten at the hotel?" Mr. Hamilton looked at Cindy.

"Yes. Ten will be fine."

Her boss walked out of the library, and Cindy sunk onto a chair and buried her head in her hands. She wasn't sure if she felt sorry for Camille… surely Mr. Hamilton would have something to say about a past due bill in that amount. Or maybe he'd just pay the bill for her and say nothing.

She rose slowly and went out to find Jamie. She needed to talk to him. She was still shaken from the whole awkward encounter. As she crossed into the lobby she saw Camille and Mr. Hamilton entering the lobby from the bar. Cindy wished she could backtrack and slip back into the library without being seen.

No such luck.

Camille looked at her and shot Cindy an angry glare. She stalked past her without a word.

Well, that answered that question. Mr. Hamilton had shown the bill to Camille.

The walk had done little good for Susan's mood. The feeling of overwhelming sadness and loss still swirled around her, along with her dread at breaking the news to Jamie. She pushed through the doors from the deck and headed to the lobby. Adam, Jamie, and a man dressed in a suit that had seen better days stood by the reception desk. She paused and gathered her strength. It was time to take Jamie aside and tell him about the letter from the bank.

Adam's face lit up when he saw her enter the lobby and she couldn't help but notice the answering flutter of her heart.

Jamie saw her and lifted a hand in a small wave. "Mom, this man is looking for you."

She walked up to the man and extended her hand. "Susan Hall. And you are?"

The man shook her hand. "Max Simons. Do you have a moment to talk… in private?" He looked pointedly at Jamie and Adam.

"I'm not sure what you have to say that can't be said in front of my son, but my office is this way." She led the way into to her office tucked off to the side of the lobby.

"Mind if I close this?" Mr. Simons motioned towards the door.

She nodded. She wasn't sure why the man was being so secretive, but she wished he'd just get to it. She still needed to sit down with Jamie and tell him about the investor calling their secondary loan.

She stood beside the desk and looked expectantly at Mr. Simons.

"I… ah… I have some news for you and some questions." He pulled out a badge from the breast pocket of his suit coat. "Detective Simons."

She glanced that the badge, more confused than ever. "Detective, what's this about?"

"You were married to Russell Burns, correct?"

"Yes. We're divorced now."

"And this is your marriage certificate?" He held out a paper.

She looked at it and nodded. A frown creased her face. *What was this all about?*

"I'm part of a joint investigation into Mr. Burns. As part of the investigation, we've looked into his financial dealings. He's been involved in some questionable activities. I'll leave it at that until anything official happens."

"Doesn't surprise me. Nothing Russell does surprises me anymore."

"In our investigation we turned up a hidden account. It wasn't disclosed in your divorce proceedings and it appears it is your money from before you married Russell."

"I had a small trust fund set up by my grandfather. Russell insisted I could keep it as my account, not community property, but it was all lost in the market crash."

"Well, I'll say one thing, the man is shrewd. He had a front company that he had you invest the money in. He had that company fail, but your funds were moved to a hidden account. They were never commingled with his funds, which actually protected them from our investigation. I wanted to come here and personally give you the information on your account. I don't take well to people cheating on their spouse and hiding funds in a divorce."

"I don't understand."

"Your account has actually grown quite a bit. The trust your grandfather wrote up is iron clad, which I assume is why Russell hadn't found a way to liquidate it yet." Detective Simons reached into his breast pocket again and drew out another paper. "Here is the information on your account."

She slowly reached out the paper and scanned it.

Oh my goodness.

She took two steps back and sank onto her desk chair. "This is *mine*?" The amount listed on the paper boggled her mind. It would pay off the secondary loan and go a long way on repairs and updates for the inn.

"Yes, ma'am. It is. There will be a bit of paperwork to fill out to get it, but I put the name of our forensic accountant on there if you have any problems at all. Looks like Russell did you a favor by hiding the account, because the funds won't be included in our investigation."

"Russell did me a favor…" Susan smiled wryly. "Bet that's going to make him angry."

Detective Simons took off his glasses and wiped them with a handkerchief. He placed them back on his leathered face and then looked at her. "I do ask that you not contact him. The warrants are with the judge. As soon as he signs them—and he assured us he would—we'll have warrants out for his arrest, and as soon as they find him, they'll pick him up."

"Russell is getting arrested?"

"He is, ma'am."

"I don't even know what to say."

"The man is a cheat and a cad. You could say that karma has a way of coming back to get those who deserve it."

Susan jumped up from her chair and went around to the detective. "Detective Simons, I'm going to give you a hug, if you don't mind. You have no idea what you have given me here."

The stodgy old man actually blushed. "Just doing my job, ma'am."

She gave him a quick hug.

"Well, I best be going. Got a lot of paperwork to do now that the case is wrapping up."

"Thank you so much, Detective."

The man left the office, and Susan stood leaning against the desk in a daze. Jamie came rushing in. "What was all that about?"

She just handed the paper to Jamie. "We've been saved."

Susan and Jamie walked arm and arm out to the lobby. She couldn't stop grinning. Russell's shenanigans had been her salvation. She'd promised to tell Jamie everything, but she wanted to explain it all to Adam, too.

Adam came rushing up to them. "Everything okay? Must be by the look on your face."

"Everything is perfect. Oh, Adam, everything is going to work out."

"That's what you think." Russell stood in the doorway of the lobby. "I came here to personally give you the papers on calling in your secondary loan. I know you don't have the funds to pay it back. I'll make you an offer of half what I offered before, or I'll wait until the bank forecloses on the inn. Your choice. But, either way, it will be mine." Russell stood with his usual Cheshire smile plastered on his face.

"I'll have the funds." Susan walked up to him and stood toe to toe.

"Dream on. You don't have the money." Russell shook his head. "Last chance on my offer, or you can lose every last penny you put into this place."

Jamie came and stood by her side. "You know, Russell, I think you should leave."

"I'm going to tear the place down, you know. Every last bit of it. I knew you'd never make a go of it, boy."

"Not a boy. Not your son. I'm nothing to you," Jamie growled.

All of a sudden there was a commotion in the doorway behind Russell. Four men poured through the doorway.

Detective Simons stood with an almost-smile on his face. "Ma'am." He nodded at her and turned to Russell. "Mr. Burns, you are under arrest."

"What are you talking about?" Russell glared at the detective.

"I have a warrant for your arrest."

"You're crazy."

Detective Simons turned toward another man with him. "Agent, read him his rights."

"What is this nonsense? Leave me alone. I'm going to call my lawyer." Russell's face turned bright red and he glanced around as if looking for an escape route.

"That would be a good idea, sir. You can call him from the station."

Susan watched in awe as they handcuffed Russell and two of the men led him away. Detective Simons turned to her and smiled. "Lucky coincidence I was here when the warrants came through. Made my day to be part of his arrest. You take care, ma'am."

"Thank you, Detective." The man left with a bit of spry spring in his steps.

"Mom, I think you have some explaining to do." Jamie titled his head to one side as he watched the last of the men leave.

"And I need to talk to you, Susan." Adam came up to her and touched her elbow. "I have some good news. I think I have a way to save the inn. Two ways, actually."

Jamie and Susan laughed, and Adam looked at them strangely.

Susan hugged Adam quickly. "It seems to be the day for good news."

~

That night Adam and Susan sat on the deck. Clouds covered most of the sky, but every once in a while the moon would peek out from behind the clouds and throw a shaft of light across the water.

He held her hand while they sat. He knew their days together were numbered, and he cherished every last moment he had here with her.

"I can't believe you found those old stock certificates. I had no idea they even existed." Susan smiled. "It's been quite the day."

"And my buddy at the company assures me they are valid certificates. Looks like you're coming into some good money."

"I'm not sure I'll know how to act if we're not scraping by, day by day." Susan grinned.

"I bet you can get used to it."

"And you really think we can have the inn declared a historical landmark?" Susan looked a bit dazed with all the surprises the day had sprung on her.

"I do. I have someone checking into it, but if you want to pursue that, you can. It would keep the inn from ever being torn down."

"I just can't believe this day." Susan tucked a lock of hair behind her ear. "So much good news. And it looks like Russell will finally be out of my life"

"Out of everyone's life, it looks like." Adam trailed his thumb across the back of her hand.

Susan looked at him and her expression saddened. "But, you'll be leaving soon now, won't you? You've helped save the inn, just like you said you would."

"I do have to leave. I can stay another day or so. Mom is having such a good time here, I hate to take her away. But I do need to find work. There really aren't the kinds of jobs I'm good at here on Belle Island."

"I know that." Susan sighed.

The sound tore at his heart. They'd known going into this that he'd have to leave, but it didn't make it any easier.

Susan got up and slipped into his lap. He wrapped his arms tightly around her and rested his head against hers.

"I'm going to miss you so much when you're gone," Susan whispered against his cheek, her warm breath heating a fire inside him.

He kissed her then, long and thoroughly. A small whimper escaped her.

"I will miss you too." He whispered back.

CHAPTER 27

Adam couldn't put off leaving much longer. He decided to take Susan out to eat at Magic Cafe, followed by a long after-dinner beach walk. He had a few leads on jobs, one back in Atlanta and one in Chicago. He'd been stalling for days, not wanting to leave. He'd worked with the company in Chicago before, and they'd all but promised him the job. They had great benefits and the pay was a raise from what he'd been making. They'd even offered a signing bonus. All the things he needed in a job. Except for the fact it was miles and miles away from Susan.

"You look lost in thought." Susan stood before him in a simple dress and sandals. He couldn't imagine anyone looking so beautiful.

"You look amazing."

Susan blushed. "You're so good for my ego."

He stood and took her hand. "I'm ready if you are."

They walked outside and he stopped her. "Go stand by the railing. I want to get your picture."

"I… okay." Susan walked over to the railing and self-consciously tugged on a curl.

He grabbed his cell phone and captured a few quick photos. At least he'd have a picture of her to replace the boring generic one his phone sported now. He smiled at her. "Thanks."

They headed down the beach to Magic Cafe. Tally had a table by the edge of the deck waiting for them.

"You two have fun." Tally left a menu for Adam and walked away to seat some other people.

They ordered, and silence descended upon them. Adam didn't know what to say. A heaviness wrapped around his heart, squeezing tightly. He hated being forced to choose between staying with Susan or taking a job where he could support his mother and take care of her. And, there really was no decision to be made, because his mother wouldn't be able to take care of herself for very much longer.

Rock, meet hard place.

"It's difficult, isn't it?" Susan's words interrupted his thoughts

"What?" He looked at her.

"It's tough being with you, knowing that it's ending soon."

"I was going to tell you after dinner, but since you brought it up, I'm going to leave tomorrow. I'm almost one hundred percent sure I'm going to take a job in Chicago. I'll need to get packed and moved and get Mom settled. I'll need to find someone to drop in and check on her. I can't keep putting it off."

"I know." Susan's voice was low. "We knew it was coming. I've had such a good time spending these last few days with you."

His heart thundered in his chest like a runaway boulder crashing down a mountain. He wasn't sure he could breath. One look at Susan's face told him all he needed to know. She was feeling the exact same way.

And he was the one putting that look on her face.

Susan was certain if you looked up the definition of broken heart, there would be a picture of her. She

could barely draw a breath and just played with the food on her plate. Her world was crumbling around her. Well, not the owning the inn part of her world, but Adam had become so important to her in such a short time. She was going to miss Mary, too.

Things would be so different with both of them gone. It's not like they could do a long distance relationship, because Adam wouldn't want to leave Mary alone in Chicago, and Susan had to run the inn, and Mary didn't need the constant confusion of traveling back and forth with Adam.

They had to do what was right for Mary.

"Will you excuse me for a moment? I need to go to the ladies' room." Susan set down her napkin and got up from the table. She was so close to tears that she needed a moment to pull herself together. She didn't want Adam to see her cry.

Tally stopped her as she went inside. "Are you okay?"

"I'm… not. Adam is leaving tomorrow. I just don't know what I'm going to do."

"Ah, I'm so sorry." Tally gave her a hug.

"I'm going to miss him so much. But it's my own fault. I knew going into this that he needed to leave."

"So ask him to stay." Tally gave her a listen-to-my-advice look.

"I can't ask him that. He needs to go. He already has a job offer in Chicago that will work out great for him. Great benefits. He'll be able to take care of his mom."

Tally shook her head. "You always were the stubborn one, always putting everyone else first. Maybe you *should* ask him to stay. Hire him at the inn if nothing else. Marry him. But for Pete's sake tell him you love him."

Susan stood in shock at Tally's forthright words. "Marry him?"

"You love him, don't you?" Tally cocked her head to one side.

"I do love him." She finally admitted it to herself and to Tally.

"Then you should tell him."

"I think it will only make it that much harder. I can't ask him to choose between me and his mother."

"Throwing away love is a foolish move." Tally shook her head and walked away.

Susan was more confused than ever. She couldn't ask Adam to marry her and stay in Belle Island.

She didn't even know if he loved her.

CHAPTER 28

Susan sat at the table in the cottage the next morning, having a quick breakfast with Jamie and Cindy.

"You're sure quiet this morning." Jamie eyed his mother.

"I'm sorry. I know I'm not very good company."

"You don't have to be any certain way with us." Cindy reached across the table and squeezed her hand. Jamie loved the way his wife was so kind to his mother. He smiled to himself. He loved *everything* about his wife.

Susan looked at him. "It's just that Adam and Mary are leaving this afternoon."

Jamie shot her a piercing glance. "He's leaving? I

231

almost figured he'd stay. Mom, it's obvious that you care about him and he cares about you."

"Well, he got a job offer in Chicago. Good pay and benefits. He'll be able to take care of Mary."

"But what about you and him?" Jamie set down his mug. "You should work something out."

Cindy jumped up from the table. "I've got to make a phone call."

"Now?" Jamie frowned, it wasn't like her to put business over family, and this was obviously a hard time for his mom.

"Right now... it's something... it's important. I just remembered. I'm sorry, I'll be right back." Cindy hurried into the other room.

Jamie turned back to his mother. "Did you ask him to stay?"

"Now you sound like Tally."

"Tally is a wise woman. I could do worse than give the same advice she gave."

"She said I should ask him to stay..." His mother looked up and a hint of blush flushed her cheeks. "She said I should ask him to marry me..."

"Told you she was wise."

"I don't even know... I don't know if he loves me or not."

"You love him, don't you?"

His mother sighed a long sigh that seemed to

come from deep inside of her. "I do love him."

"Did you tell him?"

Susan eyed him suspiciously. "Have you been talking to Tally?"

"No, but it appears that she and I are on the same page with this."

Cindy came back into the kitchen with a smile firmly tucked across her face. Before he had a chance to ask what was going on, he heard a knock at the cottage door and got up to answer. Dorothy walked in. "Adam was looking for you, Susan. I think he and Mary are about ready to leave. I'm going to miss Mary. It's been great having someone here that likes to knit and do the crosswords with me. I think she really enjoyed helping around the inn, too."

"You need to stall him," Cindy insisted.

"What?" Jamie looked at his wife like she'd lost her mind.

"Stall him. He has to stay for another thirty minutes or so." Cindy touched his arm. "Trust me."

Of course he trusted her, he just didn't know what she was up to.

"I need to talk to Adam anyway." Susan put down her napkin and got up from the table.

"You'll make sure he stays for half an hour?"

Susan frowned slightly. "I will."

~

Susan found Adam standing on the deck, staring at the ocean. She watched him for a minute, memorizing every detail. His broad shoulders that were so easy to lean on. His brown hair ruffled in the breeze. His strong hands resting on the railing. She let the image imprint on her mind.

He turned then, as if he had felt her watching him. A sad smile crossed his face. She walked over and stood beside him at the railing, leaning slightly against him.

"A beautiful view, isn't it?"

He looked at her. "I'll miss it."

She wasn't sure if he was talking about the ocean view or her. She couldn't bear to think of him leaving and the huge hole it would leave in her life.

A bird swooped by, and she followed its flight until it disappeared in the distance, gone forever.

She spun to face Adam full of resolve. "Adam, there's something I want… I *need* to tell you."

"What's that?" He lifted her face up to look directly into her eyes.

"Adam, I love you." There she said it. Her heart knew she'd done the right thing.

His sad expression when he heard her words caused her heart to tumble.

He didn't feel the same way.

He reached out and touched her check. "Ah, Susan. I love you, too. I think I have from that first day we were out at Lighthouse Point."

"You love me?" She needed him to say it again.

He grinned. "I do love you."

She sighed. "That's good."

"It is?"

"Yes, because it's going to make it easier to ask the next question."

A lazy grin crossed his face. "And what would that be?"

"I want to ask you if you'd stay here... and marry me."

His eyes flew open wide. "You're asking me to marry you?"

For a moment she wanted to step back and pull back the words. But Tally was right. You need to take a chance with love. She'd never forgive herself if she didn't at least ask him.

"I love you. I do. I would love to stay here and marry you... though, to be honest, I wish I had thought to ask *you* to marry *me*. But it doesn't change the fact that I have no job here. No way to take care of my mom."

"We could work that out." Susan stood before him, holding her breath, waiting for an answer.

"We have worked out a lot of problems in our time, haven't we?"

"We have."

Adam smiled and dropped to one knee. "Susan, will you marry me?"

She threw back her head and laughed. "I will." She leaned down and kissed him.

He stood and wrapped his arms around her. "Didn't want you to be the only one proposing today."

They turned at the sound of people approaching. Jamie, Cindy, and Delbert Hamilton crossed the deck.

"Adam, glad I caught you before you left. I need to talk to you." Mr. Hamilton reached into a folder he was carrying and handed Adam a paper. "Cindy here says you're out of a job right now… well you found one with Sunderland and Steadman in Chicago. You don't want to accept that offer. You want to accept mine. If you could manage the opening of The Hamilton in Sarasota, then I'd like for you to handle negotiations on buying The Beverly in Tampa. I know you've managed hotel transitions before and I know you've outsmarted me in negotiations. We can iron out the details, but the main points are listed there. Oh, and we have great benefits. I'd love to have you join us."

Adam glanced at the paper and a wide grin spread across his face. "Looks like a fair offer to me."

He turned, swooped Susan up, and spun around with her. "Looks like everything is going to work out."

Adam turned to Jamie. "Oh, and I'm hoping you'll be my best man when I marry your mother."

Cindy let out a little squeal and hugged Susan. Jamie came over, hugged her, and whispered in her ear, "I'm so very happy for you."

Dorothy and Mary came walking across the deck. "What's all the commotion over here?" Mary asked.

"Mom, I'd like you to meet my future bride."

Mary clapped her hands. "You're going to marry Susan? I always knew you were a smart boy."

"Congratulations." Dorothy grinned. "I knew it. Just knew it."

"I'm going to call Tally and Julie and tell them to come over. Let's celebrate with Champagne." Jamie offered.

"That sounds like a lovely idea, son." Susan's heart soared as Adam wrapped an arm around her waist and led her inside to celebrate, surrounded by the people they loved most.

CHAPTER 29

Susan stood in front of the full-length mirror in a suite at the inn. Julie fussed with Susan's hair, trying to tame it into submission. Tally handed her a bouquet of simple white hydrangeas.

"Do I look okay?" Susan stared in the mirror at the simple off-white suit she'd chosen to wear.

"You look lovely." Tally patted her arm. "And the weather cooperated, too. I thought for sure we'd have to move the wedding inside, but look at this warm November day."

"It sure didn't take you long to pick a date and get married." Julie laughed. "I have our wedding date, but still don't have everything planned. Reed said he was jealous of Adam for getting his wedding so quickly."

"There didn't seem to be much reason to wait. I love him. I want to be his wife." Her heart danced around in her chest with the excitement of the day, and she could feel the flush on her cheeks.

"So you and Adam and Mary will all live in the cottage?" Tally asked.

"Yes, but we're going to build a mother-in-law suite off the cottage to give all of us our space. We want Mary with us, though." Susan turned to catch her reflection in the mirror again. "And Jamie and Cindy are living in a suite at the hotel this winter, until Julie marries Reed this spring. Then they are going to rent her cottage."

"It sounds like everything turned out exactly how it needed to. See, I told you that you should listen to Tally's advice. Always." Julie grinned.

"Well, I give good advice." Tally said the words as if it should be obvious to everyone. "Are you ready?"

Susan took a deep breath. "I am."

Julie hugged her, and the three friends walked downstairs to where Adam was waiting outside under the wedding arch to marry her.

The music started. Tally and Julie walked down the aisle and stood to one side of the arch.

Jamie came and took his mother's arm. "I'm

doing double-duty walking you down the aisle and being the best man."

She tucked her hand on his arm. She couldn't imagine a better person to walk her down the aisle to her future with Adam.

She turned the corner and saw the moment Adam noticed her. His eyes filled with tears. She walked the few steps to the archway. Jamie kissed her cheek and went to stand beside Adam.

"You look beautiful." Adam whispered to her.

Adam took her hand in his strong one. They recited their vows and became husband and wife.

Adam leaned over and kissed her, the most emotional, gentle, strong kiss she'd ever imagined. He squeezed her hands. "We did it."

"Together we can do anything." Susan looked up into her husband's sparkling eyes, brimming with love, and stood on tiptoe and kissed him again.

The Unexpected Wedding - Book Five

The Wedding in the Grove (crossover short story
between series - Josephine and Paul from The Letter.)

LIGHTHOUSE POINT ~ THE SERIES

Wish Upon a Shell - Book One

Wedding on the Beach - Book Two

Love at the Lighthouse - Book Three

Cottage near the Point - Book Four

Return to the Island - Book Five

INDIGO BAY ~ a multi-author series of sweet romance

Sweet Sunrise - Book Three

Sweet Holiday Memories - A short holiday story

Sweet Starlight - Book Nine

Made in the USA
Coppell, TX
27 June 2020